"I can't have an affair with you."

Kathy had never felt so desolate in her life. "I can't do it without some sort of commitment," she finished wearily.

"'Commitment'?" Lucas echoed incredulously. "All right, forget that I ever made the suggestion. I have a spare bedroom, and you're welcome to it. Now does that make it easier for you to accept my hospitality while you decide what to do about Seaview?"

"But you said that last night, too, and look what happened then," Kathy argued, even though she knew she couldn't stay at Seaview the way the vandals had left things. "I don't want everyone in the village thinking I've become a member of your harem!"

Lucas's eyes flashed angrily, and he stepped toward her menacingly. "You're not going anywhere until we've had this out!"

Books by Flora Kidd

HARLEQUIN PRESENTS

HARLEQUIN ROMANCE

These books may be available at your local bookseller.

Don't miss any of our special offers. Write to us at the following address for information on our newest releases.

Harlequin Reader Service
P.O. Box 52040, Phoenix, AZ 85072-2040
Canadian address: P.O. Box 2800, Postal Station A,
5170 Yonge St., Willowdale, Ont. M2N 6J3

FLORA KIDD

the arrogant lover

Harlequin Books

TORONTO • NEW YORK • LONDON
AMSTERDAM • PARIS • SYDNEY • HAMBURG
STOCKHOLM • ATHENS • TOKYO • MILAN

Harlequin Presents first edition January 1986
ISBN 0-373-10848-6

Original hardcover edition published in 1985
by Mills & Boon Limited

CHAPTER ONE

'MR MACBRIDE, Mrs Kathy Reid is here to see you.'

Agnes Murray, secretary to the firm of Kelvin, Morris and MacBride, solicitors and estate agents, made the announcement loudly after she had opened the door of an office and had looked into the room. Then she turned back to Kathy, indicated that she should enter the room and whispered,

'Go right in. And the best of luck! He isn't in a good mood at all.'

Kathy stepped into the room. The door closed behind her. She stood still for a moment looking across the width of the room to the window. A man stood there with his back to her as he looked out of the window. He was fairly tall and broad-shouldered. She waited, trying to suppress a quiver of excitement. Would he remember her? When he turned around and saw her would he recognise her?

The room was furnished with a wide desk, a big leather swivel chair and several other straight chairs. Glass-fronted bookshelves lined one of the walls and every shelf was crammed with thick leather-bound books. The top of the desk was bare except for a plain foolscap folder. Realising that the silence was stretching out tensely and that the man hadn't turned to acknowledge her presence, Kathy cleared her throat impatiently, advanced towards the desk and dropped her heavy nylon holdall to the floor.

'Mr MacBride,' she said clearly and crisply, 'I'm sorry I'm a few minutes late for our appointment, but you see, the bus from Dumfries was running behind schedule. Could we get the matter of my taking possession of Seaview Cottage done now? I'd like to go to Redcliffe this afternoon and move into the cottage.'

He turned then, slowly, and faced her across the desk. He looked straight at her, his dark blue eyes—they seemed almost black—showing no glimmer of recognition. His lean face was all interesting lines and prominent bones, not perfectly handsome, but unforgettable, and now his once jet-black hair was tinged with grey at the temples. In his well-cut dark grey business suit, light grey shirt and dark blue tie he looked coolly self-contained, a poker-faced lawyer confronting a rather impulsive, headstrong client.

'Good afternoon, Mrs Reid,' he said smoothly. 'Please sit down.'

His coolness set her at a distance. Had he really not recognised her? Had he forgotten her? Feeling a little piqued because he was treating her with such polite indifference, Kathy sat down in the chair on the opposite side of the desk from him. When she looked across the desk he was seated in the big leather chair and was opening the folder.

'I'm assuming that you received the letter I sent to Andrew Reid of 217 Lilac Avenue, Edmonton, Alberta, Canada, on March the first of this year,' he said in businesslike tones.

'Yes, I did. But I told your secretary that when I phoned her for this appointment. The letter arrived after Andrew's death.'

He flashed her a sharp under-browed glance.

'Couldn't you have written to me immediately informing me of his death?' he demanded coldly.

'I knew I would be coming to Britain to stay with my parents in Manchester, so I thought I would come to see you to tell you of his death instead of writing. You see, under the terms of Andrew's will Seaview is now mine. He died six months ago and his will has been proved. He left the cottage to me and now I'm going to live in it.'

Frowning heavily, he gave her another swift under-browed glance. She had the impression that he was extremely irritated by her announcement.

'First things first,' he said curtly. 'Before you can take possession of the cottage I have to ascertain that you're really the person you say you are and that you were legally married to Andrew Reid. I'd like to see a copy of his will and something from his Canadian lawyer stating that you are genuinely the beneficiary under that will and that it has been proved.'

How cold and hard he was, quite different from the young man she had known nine years ago. Then he had just finished the years of training and had passed the exams that had qualified him as a solicitor. Now he was about thirty-five years of age and an experienced lawyer, accustomed no doubt to dealing with persons who were less honest than herself.

'I have identification,' she replied, as cool as he was. Delving into her large leather shoulder bag, she took out a brown envelope and pushed it across the table towards him. 'It's all in there,' she said. 'A copy of Andrew's will, the papers proving that I now own Seaview Cottage, Andrew's and my marriage certificate, my passport.'

He picked up the envelope and took papers from it. For a while there was silence, broken only by the rustle of paper as Lucas MacBride examined the documents.

Now he would see her maiden name, thought Kathy. And maybe he will remember Kathy Warren, the young woman who had crewed for him so many times in the sailing races at Redcliffe that summer nine years ago; the eighteen-year-old girl who had just discovered the power of her femininity and the effect it had on the opposite sex. For six whole weeks he and she had been inseparable, in love with each other, in love with love . . . or so she had thought at the time.

He returned the documents to the envelope and pushed it back towards her. She put it in her shoulder-bag. When she looked back at him he was frowning down at the papers in the folder.

'Everything is in order, isn't it? The cottage is mine, isn't it?' she queried anxiously.

He looked at her, his dark eyes unfathomable, his face set in hard lines.

'Yes, it's yours,' he said shortly.

'And you're satisfied I'm really Katherine Reid, widow of Andrew Reid?' she persisted dryly.

He noticed the hint of sarcasm in her question

and one corner of his broad-lipped mouth quirked upwards in a slight smile.

'I'm satisfied you're Andrew Reid's widow and that the cottage belongs to you now,' he drawled, leaning back in his chair and surveying her from under down-drooping eyelids. 'But you didn't have to come all the way from Canada to tell me. You could have written, or had your Canadian lawyer write to me.'

'But I wanted to come. I want to see the cottage, take possession of it and live in it. You see, Andrew and I planned to come and stay in it for summer holidays when he inherited it from John Reid ... but unfortunately he became ill, seriously ill, with a form of leukaemia about two years ago and couldn't travel.' She paused to steady her voice, then asked, 'Do you have the keys to the cottage?'

'I do.'

'Then please may I have them? I'd like to go to Redcliffe this afternoon and have a look at the place.'

He leaned forward, elbows on the desk, his lean muscular hands clasped together and held in front of his mouth while his dark eyes, narrowed to slits, studied her.

'It isn't in very good condition,' he said eventually.

'That doesn't matter. I can soon put it right,' Kathy replied confidently. 'Please may I have the keys?'

He didn't move but continued to study her. For all his face was impassive, revealing nothing of his thoughts or feelings, she had the impression his mind was extremely active as he considered her request.

'How will you get to Redcliffe?' he asked.

'By bus, I suppose.'

'The bus only goes there twice a week and not today.'

'Then I'll go by taxi.'

'Jock Gibson has the only taxi in Kilburn and he's probably out already. Why not wait until tomorrow?'

'Because I want to see the cottage today,' she replied stubbornly. 'Couldn't you drive me to Redcliffe? I'd really like to move into it.'

'You won't be able to do that. It isn't habitable—there's no furniture in it.'

'But I thought it was furnished. I thought it would be just the way it was when Uncle John used to stay in it,' she argued. 'I'm determined to go there, Mr MacBride, and nothing you say is going to put me off. Please will you give me the keys?'

'All right.' Much to her surprise he changed tactics. 'If you don't mind waiting half an hour in the outer office I'll drive you down to Redcliffe this afternoon and you can see for yourself what condition the cottage is in, since you don't seem prepared to take my word for it.' His tone was acid. 'But I can't leave until after my two-thirty appointment.'

He glanced with slow deliberation at his watch. 'It is now twenty-eight minutes past two,' he said succinctly, and rose to his feet. 'If you wouldn't mind waiting in Mrs Murray's office,' he suggested.

'I'll wait.' Kathy sprang to her feet and slung

the heavy holdall over her shoulder. 'I'll see you in half an hour.'

She sat for longer than half an hour among the potted plants in Mrs Murray's office, leafing through magazines, half hearing the secretary answering phone calls and the young copy-typist clicking softly as she typed out legal documents. Lucas MacBride took his time interviewing his next client, and she couldn't help wondering if he was doing so deliberately, hoping she would get impatient and leave the office, having given up her attempt to go to Redcliffe today, hoping perhaps that she would give up her idea of moving into Seaview Cottage and living there.

Kathy's lips pursed in a stubborn expression. Nothing was going to make her change her mind—nothing! She would sit in that office until it was closing time, if need be, until Agnes Murray and the copy-typist covered their typewriters and locked everything up; until Lucas MacBride appeared.

It was nearly quarter to four when his client left and Lucas MacBride eventually came into the outer office to give instructions to Mrs Murray about a letter. Kathy made sure he knew she was there by rising to her feet and approaching Agnes Murray's desk.

'As you see, I'm still waiting, Mr MacBride,' she said sweetly. 'If it isn't too much trouble perhaps you'll take me to Redcliffe now. And please don't forget the keys to Seaview Cottage.'

He gave her a dark hostile glance and turned back to Agnes Murray to issue more instructions. When he had finished he said smoothly to Kathy,

'Please go down to the front entrance of the building. I'll drive round and pick you up there.'

He went back into his own office and shut the door. Kathy picked up her holdall, said good afternoon to Agnes Murray and found her way down the wide staircase to the high entrance hall of Kilburn Town Hall where the offices of the firm of solicitors were located. Through the double front doors she went and down the wide shallow steps to wait on the pavement.

It was a glowering gusty day at the end of May. The sky was bruised with purple clouds and on the other side of Kilburn High Street the old granite buildings glittered in the uncertain sunshine. In the short time she had been in Kilburn Kathy had the impression that it had changed hardly at all in nine years. The same shops were on the ground floors of those buildings opposite; the same butcher, the same greengrocer and the same bakery. Even the wind was the same, sweeping up the narrow street, lifting the skirt of her raincoat, blowing her longish honey-coloured hair across her face.

She was pushing her hair back for the umpteenth time when the sleek grey Jaguar car purred up to the kerbside in front of her. Lucas got out of it and came round to take her holdall from her and put it in the boot, indicating with a gesture of one hand that she should get into the front passenger seat.

Swiftly the car was driven along the High Street past old granite houses that gave way to small cottages, then fields and woods. The road to the coast wound between drystone walls overgrown with honeysuckle vines, hawthorn bushes and wild roses. Beyond the walls green hills were scarred here and there with outcrops of grey rock or crested with wind-bent Scots pines. Newly ploughed fields were dark brown. Forests were blue-green edged with silver birches tasselled with yellow catkins. A small lake gleamed purple and silver reflecting the wild windswept sky. Brown and cream dairy cattle plodded across a meadow towards a high-shouldered white farmhouse half hidden by tall elms.

'It's all so neat and small,' murmured Kathy. 'And it doesn't seem to have changed at all.'

Now perhaps he'll say something. He'll ask me when I was here before and he'll say he remembers me, she thought. But he made no comment. He didn't even glance at her. He drove on, looking straight ahead, aloof and enigmatic, behaving as if she hadn't spoken, as if she weren't there... And he hadn't recognised her, damn him! Kathy's lips tightened and she looked away from his craggily attractive profile, wishing she could be as unaware of him as he was of her, and in the distance she saw two hazy hills silhouetted against the sun-gilded rolling clouds.

'Benmain and Scarface!' she exclaimed, recognising them with a feeling of pleasure and forgetting her own irritation for a few moments. 'Once I thought they were mountains. Now they look like molehills.'

Her remark struck a spark in Lucas. He actually condescended to speak to her.

'No doubt you're comparing them to the Rockies,' he sniped. 'But to those of us who live here they are still mountains.'

'How long have you lived here?' she asked, turning to him. Nine years ago he had lived in Edinburgh, had studied law at the University there and had been articled to a firm of lawyers in that city. He had been on holiday in Redcliffe that summer. So what was he doing in the district now, practising law as a partner in a small firm of country solicitors?

'About five years,' he replied laconically.

Questions bubbled up in Kathy, longing to be asked. Where exactly did he live? Was he married now with a family? She slid a sidelong glance in his direction. Somehow she couldn't imagine the Lucas MacBride she had known married and domesticated with a young family. He had been too self-orientated, too arrogant, full of enthusiasm for his own future, ambitious and determined to be successful. Marriage and a family hadn't been a part of his plans for himself at all, she had learned that the hard way when he had ended their brief affair callously by leaving Redcliffe without a word of goodbye and never getting in touch with her again.

But to ask him questions, personal questions, would betray to him the fact that she had known him nine years ago, and she didn't want to be the first to admit that they had once been close, very close. She was determined that he should be the first to refer to their shortlived romance. He had to say he remembered her, and then she might . . . she just might . . .

say she remembered him.

The car flashed through a small village, a row of white cottages, and the tyres squealed on tarmac as it took a corner tightly, turning on to a narrower road that swooped up and then down a hill. A severe-looking church built of grey granite with a pointed finger of a steeple appeared on the right. Detached villas gleamed among hedges and shrubs, each one on its separate plot of land. At the bottom of the hill the road divided. The left fork followed the shore of a wide river estuary through the village of Redcliffe, a row of houses huddled beneath a steep escarpment. The right fork, no more than a narrow gravel lane, followed the shore of a low-lying peninsula of land that jutted out at the head of the estuary.

Swerving to the right, the car lurched along the lane past the open wrought-iron gates of a house which was hidden among rowan trees that were not quite in leaf yet. Further along the lane, almost at the end of the peninsula, the car stopped in front of a gate set in a drystone wall.

Kathy stared at the wooden gate. Eight years had passed since she had last seen it when she had come with Andrew to meet his uncle John Reid who had owned the cottage and had stayed in it during the summer months. Beyond the gate she could see the grey granite walls of the cottage. There were two windows on the ground floor on either side of a plain dark green front door. Above, in the sloping slate roof, were two dormer windows.

'So here we are,' said Lucas. 'Do you still want to see inside it?'

She glanced at his rough-hewn profile. Despite the outward trappings of respectability, the smooth expensive cloth of his suit, the crispness of his shirt collar, the gold watch half-hidden by his shirt cuff, he still managed to convey the impression of being untamed, beyond the reach of someone like herself. *Or any other woman*. And it was that remoteness, coupled with a tough muscular physique, that made him so *sexy*. . .

'I said do you still want to see inside the cottage?' His voice, roughened with impatience, broke through her wandering thoughts, bringing her back to the reality of the situation, and she saw that he was looking at her, his lips curled in an expression of cynicism.

'Yes, of course I do,' she retorted and, opening the door of the car, she got out.

Wind gusting in from the distant sea caught at her hair and whipped her raincoat skirt against her legs. It tugged at Lucas's hair too, ruffled its smoothness and flung it across his broad forehead so that for a few moments he looked younger, more like the man she had once known. He opened the gate and began to walk up the path towards the front door of the cottage. Kathy followed him. The appearance of the cottage was disappointing. With its grey walls, uncurtained windows, it seemed much more bleak than she had remembered it, stuck there as it was on the end of the peninsula close to the wind-tossed water of the estuary. Some of the shrubs and bushes in the garden looked as if they were dead, killed by neglect or by severe weather.

Lucas produced two keys, one an old-fashioned iron key, the other a Yale. He fitted the iron one into the lock of the front door, pushed the door open and entered the house. Kathy followed him eagerly.

There was a small entrance hall with a narrow staircase curving up to an upper floor. Under the staircase was a slightly open door revealing a small room with a wash-basin and lavatory. To the right was a wide room with a bay window at the side overlooking the estuary; to the left was another doorway into the kitchen.

The floor in the kitchen was made of stone flags. Under the front window was a porcelain sink, crazed with tiny cracks. On the outer wall was an old cast-iron fireplace with an oven attached to it. A bare electric light bulb hung from the ceiling and plaster had fallen from walls where damp had seeped into them. The whole room looked damp and derelict.

Secretly dismayed by the appearance and condition of the kitchen, Kathy turned to Lucas. He was leaning against the jamb of the doorway, hands in his trouser pockets, and he was watching her narrowly.

'Well?' he queried with a mocking twist to his well-shaped lips. 'Is it just what you expected?'

'No, it isn't. It wasn't like this when Uncle John lived here eight years ago,' she retorted. 'What happened to the furniture?'

'Most of it was broken or damaged in some way by the gang of toughs who lived here for about a year before John Reid died, four years ago. I got rid of it when they left. Since then the cottage has been lived in only once for about six months. It was let to the Whelans just after Andrew Reid inherited it, about three years ago. You might remember I arranged with him to let it to them.'

She did remember vaguely some such arrangement having been made, so she nodded and moved towards the doorway. He stood back so she could step into the hallway.

'I'll just look upstairs,' she said.

She mounted the narrow curving staircase. The two rooms under the roof were very similar, with sloping ceilings and dormer windows. The wallpaper on the walls of both was stained with damp and they stank with mouse dirt and mould. Leaving them with a shudder of distaste, Kathy went downstairs again. As Lucas had said, the cottage was in bad condition and possibly not fit to live in.

But she could make it fit to live in, she knew she could.

Lucas was standing at the front door looking out at the view of the hills beyond the estuary, but when he heard her footsteps he turned to look at her, one dark eyebrow raised in sardonic enquiry.

'Do you still want to move in right away and live here?' he asked.

Standing in front of him, her head up, her shoulders straight, she looked him in the eyes.

'I guess that as the executor of John Reid's estate you've been responsible for this house in Andrew's absence,' she said.

His eyes narrowed warily.

'That's right,' he replied.

'Andrew asked you to keep an eye on it for him,' she insisted. 'Is ... is this,' she waved a hand towards the dilapidated kitchen, 'is this how you've done what he asked?'

'I've kept an eye on it,' he retorted. 'But that didn't mean I had to renovate it ... unless he sent specific instructions. For over two years now I've been waiting for instructions from him, but have heard nothing until you arrived today.'

'He was ill,' she defended Andrew quickly. 'Too ill to write to you.'

'But you weren't,' he jeered. 'I guessed you wouldn't like it when you saw it again and wouldn't want to live in it. So shall we go now? I'll drive you back to Kilburn and we can discuss what you should do with the place at my office. My advice is that you should sell it.'

'Sell it?' she exclaimed. 'Who would want to buy it as it is?'

'I've had many enquiries about it,' he said, briskly businesslike. 'That's why I wrote to Andrew Reid—believing him to be still alive— asking him for the second time what he wanted me to do with it.'

'And if Andrew had come in answer to your letter instead of me would you have advised him to sell it too?' she challenged.

'Probably. Seaside property goes for good prices in Redcliffe. There's always someone looking for a cottage to buy, and while Seaview doesn't look much at the moment it could be transformed if money was spent on it.' His glance raked her appearance, her windblown hair, her creased raincoat. 'The sort of money you don't seem to have,' he added nastily.

That did it. Her head went higher and she gave him what she hoped was a scathing glance.

'But I don't want to sell it,' she replied grandly. 'I'm going to live in it. I'm going to clean it, re-paint it and re-furnish it. I'm going to renovate the bathroom and the kitchen and I'm going to live here and write my next novel here.'

'You write novels?' His glance was derisive. Scorn edged his voice. 'What sort of novels?'

'Historical romances. I've written two,' she said haughtily.

'Oh, those.' His lower lip curled disparagingly. 'All blood and thunder, rape and violence, with a bit of history thrown in.'

'Not at all!' Kathy found she was almost spitting at him with rage. 'My stories aren't violent. The accent is on romance set against a historical background.'

'Have they been published?' He was still amused in a sardonic, unkind way.

'The first was published two years ago and the second will be out next month.'

'In Canada?'

'And in the States. And the first one will soon be published in paperback in this country.' *So there*, she thought to herself. *Put that in your pipe and smoke it, Lucas MacBride!* 'I thought I would set my next novel in this district. The whole area is teeming with stories about Robert the Bruce, and it isn't far from here that Mary, Queen of Scots crossed the Solway on her way to England.

There's loads of material for a historical romance or mystery.'

'I don't doubt it,' he said dryly as they stepped out of the house and he locked the front door. 'But you'd be far better off selling the cottage and going back to Canada to live. Don't you have a house in Edmonton where you could live?'

'Not any more. Andrew and I were buying a house, but I sold it when he died. I didn't want to stay there.' She glanced back at the house. Was it possible to whitewash granite? she wondered. Or colourwash it? A warm sunshine yellow to brighten it and make it look more welcoming, with white shutters to edge the downstairs windows. 'I want to live here,' she added determinedly. 'And I'm not going back to Kilburn to your office to discuss it. I'm going to stay the night at The Moorings. It is still a hotel, I hope.'

'Yes, it is.' Lucas swung the gate open for her.

He drove her from the cottage straight into the village stopping in front of a four-storey building of granite that had a sign hanging over its doorway. The words The Moorings had been painted on the sign with a picture of a sailing ship riding to its anchor.

'This is another place that hasn't changed much,' said Kathy as she got out of the car when Lucas opened the door for her. Surely now he'll say something about us both having been in Redcliffe nine years ago, she thought. Surely he remembers we used to meet in the lounge of this hotel after racing.

But all he said was:

'If you've any sense you'll sell the cottage. I
know of someone who would make you a very
good offer for it as it stands and wouldn't have to
take out a mortgage to buy it. Think about it
while you stay the night here and let me know if
you change your mind.'

'I don't have to think about it. I've made up my
mind. I'm not going to sell it—I'm going to
renovate it and live in it, because that's what
Andrew would have liked me to do and because he
wouldn't have sold it,' she retorted, and turning
from him she pushed open the inner vestibule door
of the hotel and stepped into the entrance hall.

There was a table set against a wall and on it
was a bell. Kathy picked up the bell and rang it.
A woman appeared in a doorway at the back of
the hall and came forward. About forty years of
age, she was well-built with square shoulders and
heavy breasts. Her short black hair was wiry and
she had twinkling dark brown eyes set in a round
pink-cheeked face. She was wearing beige slacks
and a beige cotton sweater.

'Good afternoon, Mr MacBride,' she said
politely to Lucas, who had followed Kathy into
the hallway.

'Good afternoon, Mrs Travis,' he replied,
equally polite. 'This is Mrs Reid. She's here on a
visit from Canada and would like to stay the
night. Can you put her up?'

'Of course.' Mrs Travis's eyes crinkled at the
corners as she smiled at Kathy. 'Welcome to
Redcliffe, Mrs Reid. We often have visitors from
Canada and the States staying here. Some of
them come over searching for relatives. You

wouldn't be related to Mr John Reid who used to own Seaview Cottage, would you?'

'Only by marriage. My late husband was John Reid's nephew,' Kathy explained. 'I'm from Lancashire originally, but I came here twice for my summer holiday some years ago. I met Andrew, my husband, here when he was staying with Uncle John, and now I own the cottage.' She turned back to Lucas. 'Oh, that reminds me. May I have the keys, Mr MacBride, please?'

He took the keys slowly out of his pocket and stepping towards her placed them in her outstretched hand. From under down-slanting satirical eyebrows his dark eyes looked right into hers and she felt a strange tingling shock go through her. She was sure now that he knew who she was and had known all the time. For a moment of electrifying awareness they stared at each other, and Mrs Travis might as well have not been with them, for all the notice either of them took of her.

Her heart pounding, her cheeks slightly flushed, Kathy was the first to look away as she put the keys in her shoulder bag.

'I realise you were reluctant to bring me to see the cottage and I know now that you don't want me to live there,' she said in a low voice, 'but I didn't fly all those thousands of miles to be put off by damp and mould and a few mouse-droppings, or to be bought out. I'm going to live at Seaview and make it my home—and I won't be needing your services as a solicitor or as an estate agent any more. Thank you for driving me here, and for your interest in the matter.'

Lucas's eyes glinted and he gave her the benefit of his devastating corner-of-the-mouth smile, and immediately all kinds of memories of him rushed into her mind, memories she thought she had stamped out long ago; memories of being alone with him, being kissed by him, being loved by him.

'It was my pleasure, Mrs Reid,' he said softly, and turning on his heel he walked away and out of the hotel.

Kathy let out a long breath and stood for a few moments staring at the closed door, suppressing a strong impulse to go after Lucas and tell him who she was; to force him to admit he remembered her and their brief romantic affair. Romantic for her it had been, she reminded herself ruefully, but possibly for him it had been nothing more than an ephemeral summer affair, a purely physical thing brought on by propinquity and reaching its highest and most romantic point when they had sailed by moonlight to a remote, secluded bay and had spent the night together.

'Mrs Reid, would you mind filling out this card and then I'll show you to your room.' Mrs Travis's voice spoke behind her and she jumped, startled out of her reverie.

'Yes.' She picked up the pen and filled out the card.

'Are you really going to live at Seaview?' asked the hotel-keeper curiously.

'I intend to, once I've cleaned it up, painted it and furnished it.' Kathy signed the card. 'But I'll need help, I'll need to find tradesmen to overhaul the plumbing and repair the roof and to do some carpentry. But right now I need to know where to buy paint and furniture.'

'Do you have a car?'

'No.'

'Then you're not going to find it easy to get about,' said Mrs Travis practically. 'You'll have to go to Kilburn for tradesmen and cleaning and painting supplies and to Dumfries or Castle Douglas for furniture, and the bus only goes to Kilburn twice a week.'

'Would I be able to buy a small car in Kilburn?' asked Kathy, slinging her holdall over her shoulder and following Mrs Travis to the stairs.

'Now that I canna say.' The hotel-keeper began to go up the stairs. 'But Harry, my husband, will tell you more about cars than I can. I'll ask him to have a word with you while you're having supper tonight, if you like.'

'Yes, I would like. What time will you be serving supper?'

'About half-past six. The season for the hotel hasn't started yet and you're our only guest, so it won't be dinner, more like high tea.'

'That's fine.' They had reached the top of the first flight of stairs and were going along a narrow corridor. Outside one of the doors Mrs Travis stopped, took a key from her pocket and unlocked the door.

The room was small but comfortably furnished with a single bed, an armchair, two chests of drawers, a wardrobe and a wash-basin. The view from the window was over the village road and the sea-wall to the river estuary, gleaming gold in the suddenly bright sunshine, and the mountains beyond.

'I hope ye'll be comfortable,' said Mrs Travis.

'Oh, I shall. It looks very nice,' said Kathy, turning back from the window.

'Ye'll have to share the bathroom on this floor with three other rooms, but since there is no one staying in them ye'll have it to yourself for tonight,' said the hotel-keeper, who seemed to be extremely friendly and communicative.

'I'll probably be staying more than one night, if that's possible,' said Kathy. 'I'd like to stay until the cottage is fit to live in.'

'No problem there,' said Mrs Travis cheerfully, and moved towards the door.

'Mrs Travis——' Kathy began, and the woman paused to look back.

'Polly,' she said. 'Please call me Polly—everyone does who stays here. Now what were you going to say?'

'You wouldn't know why Mr MacBride doesn't want me to live at Seaview, would you?'

'Now whatever makes you think he doesn't want you to live there? Has he said so?'

'No. But he tried his best to prevent me from coming to see it, and then he advised me to sell it.'

'Well now,' Polly frowned consideringly. 'It could be because there's talk that it's haunted,' she murmured.

'Haunted! You mean it has a ghost?' exclaimed Kathy.

'Aye. More than one—two, in fact. Two smugglers who killed one another when they were living there. They're supposed to walk about in the garden at night.'

'Regularly? Do they come at a set time every night or once a week or a month?' asked Kathy, her novelist's imagination intrigued by the suggestion of ghosts.

'Now I canna be sure of that,' said Polly . 'Mrs Whelan who used to live at Seaview for a while can tell you more about them than I can. But that could be one reason Mr MacBride suggested you should sell it. On the other hand, it could be that he wants to buy it himself from you.'

'But why would he want to do that?'

'Well, it blocks his view of the river. He lives at Rowans, the house behind Seaview. Ye ken the house I mean?'

'Yes, I do. It used to belong to some people called Hendry,' said Kathy, amazed by the information. So that was why Lucas didn't want her living at Seaview. She would be too near him, and he probably had a wife and family and wouldn't want to be explaining to them about his affair with her if he had remembered her, and she was sure now that he had. 'I suppose his family lives there too,' she added.

'He doesna' have a family,' said Polly. 'Or if he does they don't live with him. He could be married and separated, or he could be divorced. Or he could still be a bachelor for all I know. He doesna' talk a lot about himself. He's a wee bit dour and unsociable, ye might say. Keeps to himself. You'll excuse me now, Mrs Reid—I must away to get Harry's tea ready before the bar opens. I'll see you later.'

Alone in the room, Kathy wandered over to the window again and looked out at the sunlit water of the estuary. In the part of the river channel they had always referred to as the Deep Pool three yachts were moored. Two were white and one was blue. All were sailing cruisers with cabins and tall glinting masts.

Lucas lived at Rowans. Lucas would be her nearest neighbour when she lived at Seaview. Lucas, who had been her first, never-to-be-forgotten lover, over whom she had shed bitter tears and whom she had tried to forget in her marriage to Andrew, would be her close neighbour. She laughed a little drearily at the irony of the situation. In doing what she believed Andrew would have wanted her to do, in coming back to Redcliffe, she seemed to have come, emotionally speaking, right back to the beginning. No wonder Lucas didn't want her to live at Seaview!

And wasn't it possible that if she had known he lived at Rowans, if he had told her they would be close neighbours, she would have followed his advice and sold the cottage?

CHAPTER TWO

NEARLY two weeks later, on a Friday afternoon at the beginning of June, Kathy stood on a table in the kitchen at Seaview Cottage and applied ivory-coloured paint to the ceiling. She had already painted one of the upstairs rooms which she intended to use as a bedroom for herself and she hoped to finish painting the kitchen and the bathroom over the weekend. On Monday the furniture she had chosen for the two rooms would arrive and she would move in. The rest of the painting could be done while she was living in the cottage.

She was pleased with progress so far, but realised she could not have done much without the help of Polly and Harry Travis. Harry had driven her into Kilburn and had helped her to find a small car to buy. He had also introduced her to a plumber who had installed new bathroom furniture and a new sink in the kitchen. He had recommended a roofer and a plasterer, both of whom had been most obliging and quick to do repairs to the roof and the walls. Now all that needed to be done was the decoration. Polly had helped her to clean, to scrub walls and wash windows and would be coming on Monday to help with the installation of the furniture.

Yes, she was really glad she had stayed, and she was feeling sure she had done the right thing in refusing to sell the cottage. The recent two weeks of activity, of planning how to renovate the cottage, had done wonders for her outlook on life. The traumas associated with Andrew's long illness and his death were fast receding from her mind and she had slept well every night since she had arrived in Redcliffe.

A sharp knock on the door of the kitchen startled her. She stopped painting, stepped back, and collided with the can of ivory paint, knocking it over so that thick creamy paint spilled across the table and began to drip on to the floor.

'Oh, damn! Now look what you've made me do!' she exclaimed, glaring at Lucas MacBride, who was standing in the doorway. 'Why didn't you knock on the outer door. . .'

'I did, but you didn't answer, so I walked in,' he retorted.

'Well, don't just stand there,' she snapped, jumping down off the table. 'Help me stop the paint from going all over the floor. There are some newspapers somewhere—over there. I'll hold the can under the drips and you can push the paint towards it with the newspapers.'

They worked in silence until they had collected as much of the spilled paint in the can as they could. Then Lucas took the paint-soaked newspapers and cloths they had used out to the dustbin in the back garden, while Kathy washed her hands at the sink.

'What have you come for?' she asked, drying her hands on a towel while Luke washed his hands. She hadn't seen him since their last meeting and had decided he had taken notice of what she had said to him about not needing his services as a lawyer any more and had kept away from her deliberately.

'Just being neighbourly,' he replied, taking hold of the other end of the towel to dry his hands, an action that brought him closer to her than she would have wished.

Dressed casually, as if to go sailing, he was wearing jeans and a navy blue crew-necked sweater over a checked open-necked shirt. His hair was ruffled, his lean face was wind-tanned and he was a powerful physical presence in the room, so powerful that Kathy's nerves twanged unexpectedly in reaction to his nearness, and she dropped her end of the towel quickly and moved away to lean against the edge of the table.

'Why didn't you tell me we would be neighbours?' she challenged him.

'I knew you'd find out soon enough from Polly Travis,' he replied dryly.

He hung up the towel and, folding his arms across his broad chest, leaned against the sink. His dark unfathomable glance drifted over her shrunken T-shirt which didn't quite meet the waistband of her jeans and left a large expanse of bare midriff exposed. A faint smile quirked the right corner of his lips and her heart did a hop, skip and a jump. Oh, why didn't she remember how devastating that crooked smile of his could be, and why couldn't she control the leap of delight she felt when she saw it? She would have thought that the passage of time would have dimmed his masculine attraction, but it hadn't. In fact he was more physically attractive now than he had ever been, with that touch of grey in his hair and the lines graven in his lean cheeks giving his face a worn, somewhat ravaged look as if he had lived hard and rather tempestuously.

'How have you been coping with the renovating?' he asked.

'Very well, no thanks to you,' she replied churlishly. 'I'm hoping to move in on Monday. I hope you've no objections.'

'Are you going to live here alone?' he queried, ignoring her aggravating remark.

'Yes, although what business it is of yours . . .' she began aggressively.

'I only wondered if you had children, that's all,' he interrupted her coolly.

'No. No children—unfortunately,' she replied, half turning away to avoid his dark penetrating stare and thinking a little sadly of the miscarriage of her and Andrew's first baby. She had been deeply disappointed, but Andrew had taken the incident in his stride and had comforted her by taking her hand in his and saying, 'Never mind, darling. We'll have another child one day.' But she hadn't conceived again, and he had become ill. She glanced at Lucas curiously. 'Are you married?' she asked.

'I have been,' he replied, evasively, she thought, as he shrugged. His glance roved over her again. 'You've changed since we first met. How long ago was it? Nine years?'

'Oh, so you've remembered, have you?' she jeered. 'You've recognised me at last!'

'What do you mean by "at last"?' he retorted.

'I recognised you when you walked into my office two weeks ago.'

'Then why didn't you say so?'

'I was waiting for you to say something first.' His smile flickered briefly and tantalisingly. 'I suppose you were a little put out when I didn't say anything to you about us having met before and that was why you pretended not to know me,' he suggested with a mocking grin.

'No, not at all,' she replied coolly. 'I didn't recognise you at first,' she lied, annoyed by his accurate guess about her having been piqued. He knew far too much about her. Or was it rather that he knew far too much about women? 'You've changed too, you know. And then nine years is a long time,' she went on, trying to land a blow at his self-esteem, to get through that armour of amused arrogance of his. 'Much longer than the few weeks we were here on holiday that summer. Actually I find your assumption that I would want to remember or recognise you extremely arrogant and typically male. Why on earth should I remember you?'

Something wickedly hostile glinted in his dark eyes momentarily and she tensed, bracing herself for rudeness on his part.

'So you refuse to admit that you and I were lovers nine years ago,' he remarked.

'Were we? How strange. I don't remember,' she said with a little trill of laughter.

'Liar,' he accused, his voice silken with menace and lunging away from the sink he stepped towards her.

'You don't have to be abusive.' Still leaning

against the table, pretending that she wasn't at all unnerved by his approach, Kathy tilted her chin up and braved the cold glitter in his eyes.

'I wasn't being abusive. I was merely stating a truth,' he said, standing right in front of her, trapping her against the table, so close to her she could see how long and silky his black eyelashes still were, a small scar across the high bridge of his nose, the dark growth of beard stubble along the angle of his jaw and above the long provocative curve of his upper lip. 'You're lying when you say you don't remember we were lovers for a while,' he continued, and she found herself staring in fascination at the movements of his lips. 'I was your first lover. That summer was your first time, and you were very sweet and innocent and eager to learn.'

Kathy turned her head sharply so that she couldn't see his face any more and gripped the edge of the table hard with her fingers, biting her lower lip as she tried to stem the unexpected flood of sensuous memories his softly spoken words had aroused in her.

'Get out—go away! Leave me alone,' she muttered.

'Not yet.'

He took hold of her chin and forced her head to turn until she was facing him again. Against her skin his lean fingers were rough, pressing through to her jawbone. His face close to hers, he looked right into her eyes.

'It's your eyes I remember most,' he murmured. 'They're the colour of the sea on a sunny day, greyish-green with a glint of gold. They haven't changed.'

'Let go of me,' she muttered, furious because he had dared to touch her and hold her. She raised a hand to strike his hand away from her face, but he was too quick for her. Letting go of her chin, he grabbed both of her hands and, jerking her forward so that she slammed against his hard body and all the breath went out of her, he covered her lips with his in a forceful, demanding kiss, his tongue licking and stroking provocatively along the tightly closed line of her mouth.

Her neck ached, her lips stung and her crushed breasts tingled under the onslaught of that savage, bruising embrace. Then, as suddenly as he had swooped he withdrew, letting go of her so abruptly that she was glad she had the support of the table behind her.

'You seem to have forgotten how to kiss,' he taunted cruelly, his lower lip curling disparagingly. 'It would seem you haven't had much practise over the past nine years.'

'Oh, yes, you would assume that, wouldn't you, you arrogant brute!' she hissed. 'It would never occur to you that a woman might not want to respond to an uninvited embrace, to a kiss that was forced upon her against her will. I'm not eighteen and easily seduced any more, Lucas MacBride, and you'd better believe it!'

'I can believe that you're not eighteen any more,' retorted Lucas. His dark glance raked her figure, its curves shown off by the shrunken T-shirt and hip-hugging jeans. 'You've matured physically, that's obvious,' he added. He probed one lean tanned cheek inside with the tip of his tongue and his eyes glimmered with unkind mirth. 'But not emotionally or sexually, it seems,' he continued, as if he had given the matter some serious thought. 'You're behaving as if you're still a virgin and hadn't been married for seven years. Maybe your marriage to Andrew Reid was lacking in something. Short on passion, perhaps? Is that why you write historical romances—to indulge your romantic fantasies because you haven't been able to experience the real thing?'

'You ... you arrogant, cruel bastard!' she spluttered. 'Get out! Go away! I can manage very well without being pestered by a sex-starved middle-aged Lothario like you. I suppose you believe yourself to be the answer to every woman's needs. Well, you're not the answer to mine! Go away, and don't come near me again. I don't need a man in my life, and certainly not one like you!'

There was another silence. No, they weren't really silent as they glared at each other, because they were both breathing hard. Then Lucas's lips twisted wryly and the heavy eyelids dropped over his eyes, hiding their expression. Raking a hand through his hair, he turned away from her, took a few steps towards the door and then suddenly swung back and stepped towards her again. Immediately she tensed. He saw her reaction and stopped a few feet from her, his chest rising and falling as he took a deep breath, his face setting in hard, cynical lines.

'All right, relax,' he said wearily. 'I'm not

going to touch you. I had no intention of touching you when I came here today.' He laughed a little. 'I came actually to issue an invitation. I'm going sailing in a few minutes, and I thought that maybe you'd like to come. This new boat I have is bigger than *Sprite* was. It has a cabin and is very comfortable. We could leave on the ebb and be at Wreck Bay after sundown. . . .' He broke off—deliberately, Kathy guessed, insinuatingly, knowing that the mention of Wreck Bay would awaken memories.

And suddenly she was shaken by a surging impulse to go with him, to sail along the Firth in his new boat, feel the breeze in her hair, the salt spray stinging her face, hearing the chuckle of water under the bow of the boat. It was so long since she had been sailing and she hadn't known how much she had missed the activity until now.

She became aware that he had come closer to her and was watching her calculatingly, his sensually curved lips slightly parted. She smelt the scent of his wind-tanned skin and then felt the warmth of his breath feathering her cheek as he leaned towards her and whispered temptingly,

'Tonight the moon is full. It will be a moonlit sail part of the way.'

He had done this to her nine years ago. He had tempted her then and she had gone with him willingly, blinded by her adoration of him, her first love, never guessing that he would leave her the next day and that she would never see him or hear of him again.

'No!' she said firmly and loudly, and turned her back to him. 'Oh, go away—go away!'

'Kathy. . .'

'No!' She turned on him fiercely, protecting her vulnerable, impulsive heart. 'Oh, don't you understand? I don't want to go anywhere with you at any time.'

'Why not?' Lucas had stepped back and was standing up straight and frowning at her.

'Because I don't trust you. Nine years ago I went sailing with you and spent a night. . .'

'More than one,' he interjected.

'All right, more than one, because I believed that. . .' Her voice shook a little and she had to pause to control it. 'I believed that you loved me,' she continued more steadily. 'But you didn't. It was just a game to you, one you'd played before and one which, I've no doubt, you've played since. You took what you wanted from me and then you went away without a word, without saying goodbye. . .'

'I had to go, to Edinburgh for an important interview, but I came back a few days later and you weren't here,' he interrupted her. 'No one knew where you'd gone or where you lived.' He shrugged. 'I assumed that it had been just a summer affair for you, an initiation rite which you had to experience sooner or later with someone, and you chose me.'

'I came back here the next summer, you weren't here,' she pointed out rather forlornly.

'I went abroad that summer, crewing on a yacht of a friend. I didn't come back to Redcliffe until five years ago, when I learned from John Reid that his nephew had married you. I suppose you met Andrew here.'

'Yes. He was over from Canada visiting his uncle. When he went back to Edmonton we wrote to each other regularly. Then next summer he came to Manchester and proposed and we were married,' Kathy said dully.

'How very conventional of you,' he remarked. 'Did you tell him about me?'

'Now why should I want to tell him about you?' she exclaimed. 'You were out of sight and out of mind by then,' she lied. 'And come to think of it, there wasn't much to tell him about. It wasn't much of an affair we had, and it was soon over and forgotten.'

'Or so you would like to believe,' Lucas drawled tauntingly with another shrug of his shoulders, and strode over to the doorway again. 'Sure you won't change your mind and come sailing?' He turned briefly in the doorway to look back.

'Very sure. I want to finish painting.'

'All right. But don't work too hard.'

As soon as she heard the front door close Kathy climbed back on to the table, dipped the brush in the paint can and began to paint. She painted furiously for a while, swishing the brush back and forth across the ceiling, not heeding the drops of paint that rained down on her upturned face, her scarf-covered hair and her bare arms as she gave expression to the stormy emotions that the short but sharp confrontation with Lucas had aroused in her.

Eventually she became aware that she was painting without paint on the brush and started to laugh at herself. How foolishly adolescent she was being! And she had believed she was grown up now and able to withstand any amorous approaches made by any man.

The trouble was she hadn't expected Lucas to come and see her. He was the epitome of male arrogance, she thought critically, as she dipped the brush into the can of paint, assuming that he could pick up with her where he had left off nine years ago and she had been right to put him in his place. After all, she knew very little about him. He had never been her friend as Andrew had been.

Kind, placid and supportive, Andrew had been, and she had welcomed his friendship when she had first met him eight years ago, because it had helped her get over the hurt Lucas had inflicted on the vulnerable, loving eighteen-year-old person she had been then.

Short on passion, Lucas had jeered in reference to her marriage to Andrew, and she had to admit reluctantly that he was right. But then passionate love and marriage didn't always go together, she argued. Being married to Andrew had been peaceful if a little dull. Being married to Lucas would be ... oh, no, she wasn't going to tread that path again. Lucas wasn't the marrying kind.

It was well after five o'clock when Kathy had finished painting. In the mellow sunshine of the afternoon she walked slowly back to the hotel, noting that one of the boats had left the Deep Pool. The blue one had gone, and she now assumed that it belonged to Lucas. The tide had ebbed, leaving only the pool and a winding channel of water, reflecting the blue sky between the silken brown mud-banks. In the distance the sea was sun-dazzled. The light breeze was fair and she imagined that sailing on the Firth was ideal, and was surprised by a sudden sharp tug of regret because she hadn't gone with Lucas to sail to Wreck Bay and spend the night there with him.

After a bath in the hotel she dressed in a short-skirted blue dress with a low-waisted bloused top, and went downstairs to the dining room. Now that the summer season was in full swing there were several guests staying in the hotel and having dinner that evening. Sitting at a table for two, Kathy studied the other people. There was a family, parents and two youngish children, three elderly couples and one younger couple, presumably on their honeymoon because they were holding hands and gazing into each other's eyes.

With a sigh she looked at the menu, feeling lonely and wishing she was dining with a suitable companion. If she had gone with Lucas she would have dined with him, perhaps on fish that they had caught, cooking it together, sharing jokes, laughter and memories of other sailing expeditions they had taken together and afterwards sitting out in the cockpit in the moonlight, making love ... oh, forget it. Forget it. She stared hard at the menu but didn't see the written words.

'Excuse me, are you Kathy Reid?' A voice spoke near her and she looked up rather blindly at the man who was standing by the table. He was about thirty years of age, was dressed in light blue slacks and a cream leisure shirt over which he wore a beige gold jacket, and just for a moment she thought he was Andrew.

'Yes, I am,' she said, blinking.

'I'm Mike Austin, Andrew Reid's second cousin, Kathy,' he said, holding out his right hand and smiling down at her. He was of medium height, slightly built, and had a long narrow bony face. His eyes were brown and his light brown hair was curly, fairly long and attractively styled. 'I'm really pleased to meet you,' he added. 'Polly Travis has just told me you were in here and pointed you out to me. Uncle John used to talk about you and Andrew all the time.'

'Oh, I had no idea Andrew had a cousin,' said Kathy, shaking his hand. 'I'm pleased to meet you too. Won't you sit down and have dinner with me?'

'I'd like to, but I've already eaten and I'm on my way to the village hall,' he explained. 'There's a dance on tonight, the beginning-of-the-season dance for the Sailing Club. I'm setting up the amplifying equipment for the band, but when I've done that I'll come back here and perhaps we can have a drink together when you've finished dinner. Say in an hour, in the lounge?'

'I'll see you there,' she said, pleased that she wouldn't be spending the evening alone after all, regretting that she hadn't gone sailing with Lucas.

'Great!' He smiled and nodded and left the room.

Kathy was sitting in a corner of the lounge watching people, mostly members of the Sailing Club, she guessed, drinking and talking, when

Mike joined her, sliding on to the vinyl covered corner seat beside her. He asked her what she would like to drink. She chose a Drambuie liqueur and he went away to the bar at the end of the room. In a few minutes they were raising their glasses to each other in a toast.

'Here's to our better acquaintance, Kathy,' said Mike. He was, she noticed, more self-confident and at ease than Andrew had ever been in such surroundings, much more sophisticated. 'Polly tells me you're going to live at Seaview Cottage.'

'That's right. You know, of course, that Uncle John left it to Andrew in his will.'

'Yes.' He smiled charmingly if a little wryly. 'I was always hoping Uncle John would leave it to me, but I guess Andrew had more right to it, being a Reid.' His smile faded and he looked at her directly, his brown eyes sombre. 'What happened to Andrew? Was he in an accident?'

'No. He developed a particularly pernicious form of leukaemia. Nothing could be done.'

'I'm sorry, really sorry—for you, I mean, being left a widow so young. I suppose you're still getting over the shock of his death.'

'I think I'm over it now. Or at least I'm feeling much better,' she said, touched by his apparently sincere interest. 'Coming to live here is helping.' She sipped some of her drink. 'I wonder why Andrew never told me about you?'

'Because he and I never met. You see, it was only about five years ago that I found out I was related to Uncle John and visited him. I was with the band then as lead guitarist.'

'Which band?' she asked.

'The group that's playing at the dance tonight. Uncle John was really good to us. He let us live at Seaview rent-free and he helped me start up a business in Castle Douglas.'

'What sort of business?'

'Selling hi-fi equipment, video players, TV sets.' Mike edged closer to her, his eyes sparkling. 'I can give you a good deal on a TV if you want one for the cottage. Latest model—colour, remote control,' he said enthusiastically.

'But I'm not sure I want a TV,' she told him.

'Then how about a record player?'

'That's better,' said Kathy. 'I have a lot of records. They're not here yet, but they've arrrived at Glasgow with all my other belongings. They'll be here some time next week. I'm moving into the cottage on Monday.'

'I bet you've had to do a lot of renovating and painting,' he said. 'It was in a pretty bad state when the band and I lived there.'

'How long were you there?' she asked.

'About a year . . . until that hard-faced lawyer Lucas MacBride had us evicted.'

'He had you evicted?' exclaimed Kathy. 'Oh, why? Was he acting on behalf of Uncle John?'

'He said he was.' Mike's thin lips curved downwards at the corners. 'You see, Uncle John became senile and had to be put in hospital. That's when MacBride took over the running of his affairs and had us turned out.'

'Did he give a reason?'

'Oh, sure, he had a reason. He said we hadn't been paying rent. Can you believe it? Yet Uncle John had said we could live there rent-free.

Unfortunately there was nothing in writing, so we hadn't a leg to stand on in court.' Mike's lips twisted in a sour grimace again. 'MacBride wanted us out and he got us out, and it's my belief he wanted to buy the cottage for himself, but before he could do anything Uncle John died and Andrew inherited. You wouldn't happen to know, I suppose, if MacBride ever made an offer for it to Andrew?'

'He didn't make an offer, but he wrote to Andrew asking him what he wanted to do with the cottage. The letter came just after Andrew had died. Instead of answering it I came here last week to tell MacBride I had inherited the cottage from Andrew and intended to live in it.'

'I bet he was miffed,' said Mike with a complacent grin.

'Yes, I think he was. He advised me to sell it and said he knew of someone who would make a good offer.'

'And?' Mike prompted curiously.

'I refused.'

'Good for you!' Admiration gleamed in his eyes. 'I'm glad you had the guts to stand up to MacBride. He's had it coming to him for some time.' He leaned forward and said in a low voice, 'Since he came here he's been into property investment in a big way.'

'What do you mean?' queried Kathy.

'Well, you know that he and the rest of the firm are estate agents as well as lawyers?' She nodded and he went on, 'That means they know about any property that's for sale first and are able to buy choice lots for building on. They also know who is unable to keep up mortgage repayments. Lucas MacBride is notoriously ruthless and doesn't care what means he uses to get tenants or even owners out of old and dilapidated property. Then he buys the property for a song, renovates it and sells it at great profit for himself.'

'You think he wanted to do that with Seaview?'

'Right. And you'll have to be on the alert. Now you've refused to sell to him he'll be looking for other ways to get you out or to get you to give in and sell it,' said Mike. 'So be warned.'

'I am. Thanks—I'm glad you've told me about him,' Kathy said, wondering whether one of Lucas's ways to winkle lone widows to give up their houses to him was to make amorous advances to them. 'Polly says the cottage is supposed to be haunted. Did you see any ghosts when you lived there?' she asked.

For a few seconds he looked startled. He picked up his beer mug and drained it, then set it down.

'Haunted?' he repeated. 'What sort of ghosts?'

'The ghosts of two smugglers who used to live there and killed each other in a fight over loot. The Whelans, who lived in the cottage for a short time, saw them . . . or at least they saw two figures creeping about the garden at night several times. Did you see them?'

'No, I didn't see any ghosts.' Mike stared thoughtfully at his beer mug while he pushed at it with short fingers. 'But I remember Keith—he's the drummer in the band—saying that one night when he was restless and was wandering about outside he saw two figures come up from the marshes in front of the cottage and walk through the garden and into the bushes at the back. He followed them along a path which ended at the lawn at the back of Rowans where Lucas MacBride lives. He saw them disappear into MacBride's house.' Mike flashed a grin at her and lifted his shoulders. 'At the time I didn't believe Keith. He's a bit weird and sometimes hallucinates.' He sobered and leaned closer to her. 'But in the light of what I now know about MacBride and of what you've just told me maybe Keith really did see two people creeping about. Maybe they weren't ghosts but real live smugglers delivering smuggled goods to MacBride.'

'But Lucas is a lawyer. He couldn't be a member of a smuggling ring,' Kathy argued.

'Just because he's a lawyer it doesn't mean he isn't capable of breaking the law. He knows better than you or me how to break it and not be found out.'

'I suppose so,' she sighed. She didn't like the picture Mike was painting of Lucas as a ruthless lawyer who could manipulate people and laws for his own ends, but she couldn't defend Lucas. She knew so little about him, and what she knew was all on emotional and physical levels. She knew nothing of him as a business man and lawyer.

'Would you like another drink?' asked Mike.

'No, thank you.'

'Then would you like to come to the dance with me? The group are really pretty good, if a little wild at times. They make a great sound.'

'Yes, I would like to come. It's ages since I

went to a dance. Andrew didn't dance. He . . . he didn't like beat or disco stuff.'

'And yet he was the same age as me,' remarked Mike, shaking his curly head. 'Incredible! I can't imagine him not liking it.'

'What exactly is your relationship to him and Uncle John?' asked Kathy as they walked together between the tables of drinkers towards the entrance hall.

'Oh, my grandfather was Angus Reid, Uncle John's father's younger brother. He was the black sheep of the family, left home when he was only sixteen. He married my grandmother, then deserted her. My mother was their only daughter.'

'And where does she live?' asked Kathy as they stepped out into the balmy evening air. It was not yet dark, but the sun was beginning to set, flushing the sky crimson behind the purple silhouettes of Scarface and Benmain.

'She died when I was about eight,' said Mike, lightly taking hold of her right hand as they walked along the road to the end of the village. 'My dad married again. He lives in the south of England.'

The dance was not much different from dances she had attended nine years previously with Lucas, thought Kathy some time later as she danced with Mike, but although she searched the crowd she didn't see one face she recognised. The group providing the music were young men with longish hair, a couple of them with beards, and were replicas of similar groups playing for dances in most in Canada or the rest of the western world. Mike introduced her to them, and although they acknowledged her they were indifferent to her. Glancing several times at Keith, the drummer, Kathy wasn't surprised that he had seen figures in the garden at Seaview. Judging by his glazed eyes she suspected he often experienced hallucinations, and the story Mike had told her about the figures crossing the lawn at Rowans and disappearing in Lucas's house began to seem less believable to her.

Mike was a good dancer and entertaining to be with. He seemed to be well known and well liked, and by the time the dance came to an end Kathy had to admit she had enjoyed herself thoroughly.

'I'll walk you back to the hotel and then come back to take down the equipment and pack it in the van,' said Mike as they joined the crowd of people leaving the village hall.

'Oh, you don't need to go with me,' said Kathy, asserting her independence. 'It's a clear moonlit night and there are lots of people going the same way. I'll be fine.'

'You sure?'

'Of course. You attend to the equipment.'

'Then when will I see you again?' he asked, taking her arm and guiding her away from the crowd towards the stage.

'I'll call in at your shop next week to look at hi-fis,' she promised.

'Great!' He smiled at her. 'You know, Kathy, I have this feeling you and I are going to be good friends.'

'I hope we are. Good night, Mike. And thanks for bringing me to the dance.'

She was on her way towards the door and she heard someone calling her.

'Mrs Reid! Kathy Reid, I believe. Excuse me, could I have a word with you?'

The voice was clear and bell-like. It belonged to a woman with black hair that floated about her oval face in carefully casual style, who was wearing an elegant dress of white silk that moulded her perfect figure. Topaz bright eyes looked down at Kathy appraisingly.

'I'm Jane Mortimer Smith,' drawled the woman. 'I hear you're going to live at Seaview Cottage, next door to Lucas MacBride?'

'That's right.'

'I live at Clinton Hall, up the river from here. You may have heard of it.'

'I've seen it. I sailed with Luc ... I mean, with a friend up the river once, years ago, and it was pointed out to me. Are you really a Mortimer?' Seeing the woman raise suddenly haughty eyebrows, Kathy hastened to rectify her mistake. 'What I mean is, are you really descended from the Douglas Mortimer who was one of Robert the Bruce's knights?'

'Not in the direct line—that died out. But my father's ancestors were descended from old Douglas. Are you interested in local history?'

'Very much.'

'Then perhaps you'll jump at my invitation to come to tea at the Hall next Friday at three o'clock to meet some of the other women who live in the village and surrounding area,' drawled Jane.

'I'd love to come,' said Kathy, not bothering to

hide the pleasure she felt on receiving the invitation.

'Good.' Jane Mortimer Smith smiled at her, a quick flash of perfect teeth between dark red lips. 'See you at three at the Hall on Thursday, then.'

By the time Kathy left the village hall most of the people going her way were far ahead of her. The moon was full and high in a clear sky and the air was still mild, so she lingered for a few moments by the sea-wall watching the floodtide swirling silently up the estuary, covering the mud-banks.

She was just turning away when her eyes were caught by a glimmer of white. A sailing boat was coming in from the sea, its sails shimmering with moon radiance, filled by the light night breeze. It sailed right past her and rounded up into the wind, its sails fluttering as they were emptied. She couldn't see anyone pick up the mooring, but after a while the sails were lowered and the boat became one with the shadows.

Lucas hadn't gone to Wreck Bay for the night after all; he had come back, and she wondered why.

Impatiently she turned away from the wall and began to walk towards the hotel. Nothing to do with her what Lucas did or didn't do. None of her business if he changed his mind. She had to stop thinking about him. Think instead about Mike Austin who reminded her just a little of Andrew with his hope that he and she would be good friends; a livelier, more vigorous Andrew. Think about the beautiful, aristocratic Jane Mortimer Smith and the invitation to visit

Clinton Hall, where she might pick up some valuable titbits of information about the Mortimer family to be included in her next novel.

To live a full and interesting life she didn't need Lucas MacBride, she thought, as she mounted the stairs to the first floor of the hotel. She didn't need a lover, certainly not one as arrogant and demanding as he was, and she wasn't going to let him trap her into having another affair with him. She wasn't going to risk heartbreak again.

Yet, that night, she lay awake for a long time thinking about the way he had kissed her in the kitchen at the cottage and wondering what her life would have been like if she had been able to marry him instead of Andrew.

CHAPTER THREE

IT was while Polly Travis was helping her to arrange the furniture and hang the custom-made curtains that were delivered to the cottage on Monday morning, as had been arranged, that Kathy mentioned the invitation to Clinton Hall she had received.

'My goodness, you are honoured,' remarked Polly. 'She is *the* local gentry. Daughter of an earl, no less. Her father was Earl Clinton of Clinton Hall. He died a few years ago and she inherited the Hall. She's into everything around here. She's secretary of the Sailing Club, president of the Women's Rural Institute and a member of the County Council. She's really up to her neck in local politics and doing good. Her spare-time occupation is being the wife of Dr Kenneth Smith, who has a practice in Castle Douglas. You know where the Hall is, I suppose.'

'Yes, it's on the river.'

'Aye. And it looks old enough on the outside, but I'm told that inside it's really posh. Lady Jane spent thousands having it modernised. Are you going to tea?'

'That's right.'

'You'll meet a lot of local female worthies there,' said Polly dryly. 'They'll be there to give you the once-over; to have a good look at you, size you up and decide whether you're suitable.'

'Suitable for what?'

'Suitable to live in this village or the surrounding area. They don't like incomers on principle, ye ken. It's an old Scots tradition not to take kindly to strangers who come to live in our midst, especially those who buy up local houses or land. Harry is only accepted here because he's married to me, you know, and I belong here.'

'Is that why Lucas MacBride is cold-shouldered?' asked Kathy casually. 'Because he's bought up local property and sold it again at a profit?'

'Now who told you he's done that?' asked Polly.

'Mike Austin. Is it true? Has Lucas MacBride bought up old houses, renovated them and sold them again?'

'Yes, it is. And I suppose it could have made him unpopular. But the others do it too, Kelvin and Morris, and they've been lawyers and estate agents in Kilburn for years and their fathers before them,' explained Polly, stepping down from the small ladder on which she had been standing to hook up curtains to the windows. 'There, how do they look?'

'Fine,' said Kathy.

'It's wonderful what a spot of colourful paint and some curtains do for a room,' said Polly, looking around the kitchen admiringly. 'You wouldn't think this was the same room we cleaned out the week before last. If the ladies at the tea-party don't find you suitable to live here you can always thumb your nose at them and say that you're here by right of inheritance. At least you didn't buy your way like some. What did you think of Lady Jane?'

'I thought she was very beautiful and elegant and aggressive,' said Kathy.

'Aye, that sums her up pretty well. She owns a sailing boat and races it regularly. Goes for little cruises too with your nearest neighbour, MacBride. Some say he and she are having an affair right under Dr Smith's nose.'

'Now you're gossiping, Polly,' Kathy teased.

'I know I am.' Polly grinned mischievously, obviously enjoying herself. 'But they do seem to be thick as thieves, those two, and since they're both members of the Sailing Club they have plenty of opportunities for meeting.'

'Doesn't Lady Jane have any children?'

'No. She's strictly the selfish type. That's why she has so much in common with MacBride, I suspect. Have you seen him since you moved in? I bet he hasn't been over to make you welcome with a tin of biscuits or some home-made scones.' Polly chuckled in appreciation of her own rather malicious remark.

'I've seen him once. He called in last Saturday,' said Kathy distantly, and changed the subject. She had heard enough gossip for one day.

Friday afternoon was mild and sunny. Deciding she wanted to make a good impression on the other women who would be at the tea party, Kathy dressed conservatively in a plain dress made from silvery grey linen which she decorated with a red, white and black silk scarf tied about the round neck of the dress. On her feet were black high-heeled shoes and she carried a white cardigan in case the weather became cooler. She wore her hair in its usual natural waves falling down to her shoulders from a centre parting and used the minimum of make-up, noting that living by the sea in the soft air her skin had taken on a soft golden tint that was attractive.

Driving in her small car along the main road to Kilburn, she soon reached a signpost indicating that if she turned left into a narrow lane she would come to Clinton Hall. After a mile or so of bends between drystone walls, passing green meadows where cattle grazed she arrived at the Hall, a square building with battlements. Its grey granite walls sparkled in the sunshine and behind it the river was a shining ribbon winding under the overhanging branches of willows and hazels.

The stout oak door of the Hall was open. She stepped into a vestibule and was just reaching out a hand to the doorbell when the inner glass door was opened by a woman dressed in black and white maid's uniform. Kathy told the maid her name and was invited to step into the hall.

High and wide, the hall was panelled with golden wood and its floor was completely covered with thick carpeting a slightly paler tone than the walls. A carpeted staircase which had a carved wooden balustrade swept in a wide curve to a gallery that ran round three walls of the Hall.

That was all Kathy had time to see as she was ushered by the maid across the hall and through a doorway into a huge long room that had three long windows opening on to a stone terrace overlooking the river. She had an impression of several women sitting about on various sofas and chairs and of voices murmuring in polite conversation. The maid announced her name, and Lady Jane Mortimer Smith sprang to her feet and came forward to greet her, while the other women stopped talking and turned their heads to look at her.

Lady Jane's hair was once again arranged in deceptively wild disorder and she was dressed in a finely pleated skirt of gold-coloured silk with a matching blouse. A long loop of genuine pearls glimmered softly among the loose folds of the blouse which had a deeply plunging neckline.

'Nice to see you again,' said Lady Jane in her drawling voice, her sherry-coloured eyes glittering as their glance went over Kathy's appearance.

'It was kind of you to invite me,' returned Kathy politely.

'Come and meet everyone,' said Jane.

Kathy tried hared to listen and to remember the names of all the women who were introduced, but she only retained a few of them. Eventually she sat down next to a small white-haired woman who was wearing a neat suit of blue knit with a frilly white blouse and whose blue eyes had a lively sparkle and whose name was Ina Whelan.

'I'm so pleased to meet you at last,' Ina said in a soft rather fluttery voice. 'Oswald and I ... Oswald is my husband ... used to be good friends of John Reid, and he used to tell us all about Andrew of whom he was particularly fond—and of course about you too, because Andrew had met you when he was visiting John.

And then for a while we lived in Seaview Cottage, which Andrew was good enough to let to us rent from him when we were waiting for our house to be finished. We live just up the brae now, at Greengates. You must come to tea one day.'

'Thank you,' said Kathy.

'Has anyone told you that Seaview is haunted?' asked Ina.

'Yes, Polly Travis mentioned that it was.'

'You don't want to believe that story, Kathy,' said another woman who was sitting nearby. Short and square with a bulldoggish sort of face, she had been introduced as Margery Anderson. Her hair was also white and was cut short and she was wearing a rather ugly brown pants suit. 'There are no ghosts at Seaview. There were no smugglers living there at one time either—the cottage was built long after smugglers stopped coming to Redcliffe. But weren't you here a few years ago? Did you work as a part-time waitress at the hotel one summer?'

'Did you, Kathy? Really work as a waitress?' asked Jane Mortimer Smith. She was helping the maid to hand round cups of tea and plates of scones and cakes.

'Yes. It was just a summer job and earned me some pocket money. I was here the year before that too, with the Youngs. Do you remember them, Mrs Anderson? They used to rent a house called Grey Rocks along the Firth road.'

'I remember,' Margery nodded. 'He was a surgeon from Manchester—had two daughters. You were all keen on sailing. You used to crew for Lucas MacBride, didn't you?'

'Yes, I did,' said Kathy smoothly, taking the cup of tea that was being offered to her from the silver tray the maid was carrying.

'And now he's your neighbour,' remarked Margery, who lived in a big old house high on the cliff behind the village, Kathy remembered, and who could see all the comings and goings in the village and who was very rich, having been left well off by her husband when he had died. 'You must be surprised, after all these years, to find him living next door.'

'It was a surprise,' said Kathy lightly, and looking up from taking a delicious-looking cream puff from a plate being offered by Jane she felt shock tingle through her on meeting a malignant glare from Jane's glittering eyes. Quickly she changed the subject, directing it away from herself and Lucas and, turning to Ina, asked, 'What makes you think that Seaview is haunted, Mrs Whelan?'

'When we lived there we used to hear noises in the night, often on a Thursday or a Friday. We'd hear a door opening and closing and sometimes voices whispering.'

'Didn't you ever get up and investigate?' asked Kathy, aware that Jane was lingering nearby to listen in.

'Oswald did, and once he nearly caught them, but they ran off along the path through the bushes at the back of the garden. He followed them, but when he reached Mr MacBride's lawn there was no one there. They'd vanished into thin air.' Ina spoke with soft authority. 'That's why he thought they must be ghosts.'

'Lads, more likely. Roaming about, trying to break in and steal something,' said Margery scoffingly.

'Andrew—my late husband—used to stay at the cottage with Uncle John and he never said anything to me about the place being haunted,' said Kathy. 'I've only been living in the house three days, but I haven't heard or seen anyone. But then I don't believe in ghosts.'

'No? Oh, I thought you would,' said Jane. 'I thought that being a writer of romances you would believe in anything like that.'

'A writer?' exclaimed one of the other women, leaning forward. 'Are you really a writer of romances, Kathy?'

Now they were all looking at her curiously. She glanced up at Jane. The golden eyes stared back at her and the red lips curved in a rather malicious smile. There was something catlike about Lady Jane. She was all pleasant and smooth on the outside, but if touched where it hurt she would probably show her claws and scratch swiftly and viciously in attack or defence.

'Who told you I'm a writer?' asked Kathy bluntly.

'I'm not really sure,' replied Jane, still smiling. 'Could have been Lucas MacBride when we were out sailing.' The golden eyes were hidden briefly by black lashes, but still she smiled. 'Yes, it must have been him. I remember now how amused he was by the fact that you write romances.' Jane looked round at the other women and actually laughed herself, a little trill of pure scorn. 'You know the sort of book. You can pick them up in any bookstore for a few pence and escape from your everyday life to exotic places where you'll be made love to vicariously by a handsome hero. . .'

'My novels aren't just romances,' Kathy said firmly, interrupting Jane's mocking put-down of the love stories so many women like to read. 'They are historical too. I do a lot of research for them.'

Suddenly she found herself fielding questions which were shot at her from all over the room.

'Do you write under your own name?'

'What are some of the titles of your books?'

'Will we be able to find them in the public library?'

'What's it like to be published?'

'Ladies, ladies—behave yourselves! You're embarrassing Kathy. Do give her a chance.' The speaker was a well built woman of about forty years of age whose rosy face was evidence that she spent a lot of time out of doors and whose manner, as she rose to her feet, showed that she was accustomed to taking charge of meetings. Kathy remembered her being introduced as Barbara Glass, who was chairperson of a local political association. 'I think we ought to invite Kathy to the next meeting of the Women's Rural Institute, Jane,' Barbara continued. 'We'd all love to hear her talk about how she came to write, wouldn't we?' She looked round expectantly and the other women murmured their assent.

'All right, let's do that,' agreed Jane. She looked across at Kathy. 'It'll be the annual general meeting at the end of this month. Will you come?'

'I'd like to, but I'm not sure ... I mean, I'm not accustomed to talking to a group of people. I've never done it before.'

'Just be yourself and tell us how you came to write your first novel,' said Barbara. 'We'll do the rest by asking all those questions again.'

'Perhaps you'll arrange to bring Kathy to the meeting Ina, since you live nearest to her,' suggested Jane.

'I'd be delighted to,' said Ina.

'Good, then that's settled,' said Jane.

More tea was served. The conversation became more general, then, promptly at four-thirty, as if at a signal the women began to leave, saying their thanks to Jane first. Kathy offered to drive Ina back to Redcliffe so that Oswald wouldn't have to be phoned and told to come for his wife, and as they said goodbye to Jane she said,

'Did you really crew for Lucas MacBride at one time, Kathy?'

'Yes—nine years ago.'

'He's never mentioned that he knew you then.'

'Maybe he's forgotten,' said Kathy coolly. 'Goodbye, and thank you again for a lovely tea.'

Back at Seaview, as she changed out of her dress and into more casual slacks and a cotton sweater, Kathy thought about the 'tea-party'. She guessed that the invitation to give a talk at the Women's Rural Institute meant she had been found suitable by the women who had been at the party and accepted by them as a person with whom they could socialise. Yet she had received unpleasant vibes from Jane Mortimer Smith—

and all because she had crewed for Lucas nine years ago.

Why? Because it was true Jane and Lucas were having an affair? She frowned as she hung her dress in the wardrobe. She didn't like the idea of Lucas and Lady Jane being lovers. But then what business of hers was it if they were? None at all. They were adults and could do what they liked when they were together.

Even so she didn't like to believe that Lucas would deliberately steal another man's wife from under that man's nose. Not that Lady Jane was the type of woman who would have to be stolen from her husband or that she would have to be persuaded to be unfaithful to him. No, Jane Mortimer Smith was the predatory type of woman. Having met a man she wanted she would go right out and get him and never give a thought to her marriage vows.

But the less she thought about Lucas and Jane the better. It was time she started to plan her next novel. Ideas for the plot had been bubbling up in her mind for some days and if she didn't get them down on paper soon she would forget them. This evening would be a good time to type out the plan, and perhaps to start creating one or two of the characters.

She had just taken out her portable typewriter and had put it on the small desk in her bedroom when she heard a knock on the front door. Going downstairs, she opened the door, her eyes widening with surprise when she saw Lucas standing on the step. He looked as if he had just come from his office because he was wearing a light beige summer-weight suit, a cream shirt and a patterned tie.

'What do you want?' she demanded abruptly, knowing she was being rude but hoping her rudeness would offend him and he would go away.

'If I told you you'd probably slap my face,' he mocked. 'I've brought something for you.' He showed her a wide brown envelope. 'It's the deeds of the cottage. I thought you ought to have it and put it in a safe place.'

'Thank you,' she said stiffly, knowing her cheeks had flushed at the implication behind his quick mocking answer to her rude demand. He had implied that he had come to her door because he wanted her. 'I hope that ends our business association,' she added coolly.

'It does. Now we're both free to start a different association with each other,' Lucas replied. He looked past her into the hallway. 'Have you finished painting? I'd like to see what the cottage looks like inside now that it's been renovated.'

He spoke quite pleasantly and politely, but there was a glint in his dark eyes, a wicked curve to one corner of his mouth that she didn't trust. Once he was inside the house there was no knowing what he would do. He would probably attempt to kiss her again, and she was in no mood for that sort of dalliance.

'Another time,' she replied brusquely. 'I'll be having an "at home" party soon and I'll be inviting neighbours to it for sherry or cocktails. You'll be receiving an invitation. Right now I'd like to get on with my work.'

She stepped back and took hold of the door, intending to close it in his face, but before she could he stepped through the doorway to stand just inside on the doormat looking around. If she swung the door closed it would hit him.

'What sort of work?' he asked, his glance coming back to her. 'Not more painting, surely?'

'No, writing.'

'Call that work?' His eyebrows lifted in mocking surprise. 'Haven't you anything better to do on a beautiful evening like this?'

'Such as?' she countered.

'Such as having dinner with me and holding hands by candlelight. The real thing, Kathy. A romantic evening for two instead of staying at home and thinking about it, imagining it or writing about it.' He glanced at his watch. 'I'll pick you up in half an hour. Wear something pretty and feminine.'

As when he had invited her to go sailing with him last Friday she felt a sudden urge to accept, to fling caution to the winds and go with him; to experience the real thing, as he called dinner for two at some country inn; to forget that she had known him nine years ago and consequently didn't trust his motives; to pretend they had just met, had fallen in love with each other and wanted to explore the exciting possibilities of getting to know each other better.

Then she remembered the gossip she had heard about him and Lady Jane. She recalled Mike Austin's remark about him.

'No thank you,' she said coolly. 'I'm not interested in having a romantic evening with you.'

'I can assure you it would be good copy for your next romance novel,' he said, mocking again.

'I don't write romances as such,' she retorted. 'And while we're on the subject, why did you tell Jane Mortimer Smith what I do?'

'Did I tell her?'

'She says you did.'

'When did you meet her?' he asked.

'Last Saturday at the Sailing Club dance and I went to tea at Clinton Hall this afternoon. She invited me to meet some of the women who live in the district.'

Lucas's eyes narrowed and she sensed a sudden wariness in him.

'I bet that was a bore, all those women gossiping,' he jeered.

'No, it wasn't boring, and everyone was very pleasant to me.'

'Even Jane? You do surprise me,' he mocked, and swinging away from her went into the sitting room.

With a sigh of exasperation Kathy followed him.

'I thought I told you that I'm busy and haven't time to show you the house right now,' she said sharply.

He was looking around the room critically and took no notice of her remarks.

'Lucas, please will you go. You're not welcome here,' she said.

'You seem to be good at decorating and at choosing the right furniture,' he commented, his dark glance swerving in her direction. 'As if you've done it before,' he added.

'Andrew and I renovated the old house we lived in in Edmonton. We did all the work ourselves and we had a lot of fun doing it,' she replied woodenly. 'Didn't you hear what I just said?'

'Yes, I heard. But I don't believe you,' he said coolly. 'Do you miss him?'

'Of course I do.' She turned away towards the door refusing to be drawn into a discussion about Andrew with him. 'I would really like to start work,' she went on.

Lucas caught up with her in the doorway and taking hold of her arm swung her round to face him.

'I'm glad you've come to live here, Kathy,' he said softly.

His change of tactics caught her off guard, and her breath caught roughly in her throat when she saw the sensual expression in his eyes. On the bare skin of her arm his fingers moved lightly, their tips sending seductive messages along her nerves. Desire pricked suddenly within her, a raw ache somewhere low down, and her hands tingled with impulse to reach up and touch his face, draw it down to hers so that she could kiss his hard mouth, smooth the cynical lines away from it.

Then she remembered that she didn't trust him. Pulling her arm free of his grasp, she backed away into the jamb of the doorway. Hands behind her back, her head up, she retorted,

'Well, this is a change of tune on your part! I had the impression the day I arrived here that you didn't want me to live here, that you wanted me to sell the place, and I've since heard that you would like to buy it.'

His face stiffened, the harsh lines becoming deeper, and his eyes narrowed again. He stepped back from her and leaned against the other jamb.

'Where did you hear that I would like to buy Seaview?' he asked.

'Mike Austin told me.'

'Ah, so you've met the local spiv, have you?' His upper lip lifted sneeringly. 'Did he tell you his sob story of how I had him and his friends evicted from this cottage?'

'Yes, he did.'

'And how he's related to the Reid family?'

'Yes.'

'And you believed him?'

'Why wouldn't I? He is a little like Andrew to look at, and I don't believe he's a spiv.' It was some years since she had heard the slang word, but she knew it was used to describe someone who was crooked in their business dealings. 'At least, no more than you are,' she added tauntingly, remembering that Mike had suggested to her that Lucas, being a lawyer, would know ways of breaking the law and covering up. 'I found Mike very friendly,' she went on. 'He took me to the Sailing Club dance.'

'Oh, I've no doubt he was charming,' he jeered. 'And you were taken in by him just as old John Reid was. Are you going to see him again?'

'I hope so.'

'It would be wiser not to, Kathy.' He was suddenly serious.

'I don't have to take your advice, or even listen to it. You're not my lawyer any more.'

'I wasn't speaking as a lawyer,' said Lucas, 'more as a friend.'

'You and I were never friends, and we aren't friends now,' she argued.

'Then as a neighbour.'

'And I wish we weren't neighbours!' Kathy exclaimed angrily.

'Well, you can easily remedy that.' His temper flared suddenly and dangerously. 'Sell the cottage and move out. Go back to Canada. You can be sure I won't follow you there.'

Silence followed his words and Kathy realised they had been quarrelling noisily, flinging taunts at each other as if they were sworn enemies.

'Oh, I've had enough of this,' she whispered. 'Go away, and don't come back. Stay away from me.'

'No. Not while you live here.' Lucas moved towards her and there was a subtle menace in his approach and in the expression of his dark heavy-lidded eyes as their glance slanted to her lips. 'While you live here you can expect me to call on you,' he murmured, and raising a hand he took hold of a strand of her hair and tucked it behind her ear. The gentle offhand caress made her pulses leap unexpectedly and she groaned, closing her eyes so that she couldn't see him, moving her head from side to side in negation of the intention she had read clearly in his face.

'I wish you wouldn't do this, Lucas,' she protested weakly. 'It isn't fair to do this to me. You can't pick up where you left off nine years ago. Too much has happened to me ... to you ... for you to do that. We're two different people.'

'I agree with that,' he said softly, and she opened her eyes in surprise, then wished she hadn't. He was still there, close to her, his lips slanting in a slight smile. 'You're much more desirable than you were at eighteen,' he murmured.

'Stop it,' she whispered. 'Oh, stop it! Go away. . .'

Whatever else she had been going to say was lost and forgotten, smothered by the warm pressure of his lips. This time he kissed her gently, his lips exploring and stroking hers until she longed to respond. But if she did he would think she was willing to submit to his demands. She had to teach him somehow that she wasn't available. So again she kept her lips obstinately closed and held herself stiffly, pressing back against the doorjamb, drawing support from it.

Lucas raised his head, and from under down-drooping thick lashes his eyes glinted wickedly.

'I wonder how long you're going to pretend you're not interested,' he taunted.

'I'm not pretending. I don't need you, Lucas.'

'No?' One dark eyebrow flickered in satire. 'I beg to differ. You're doing your best to hide it, but inside you're blazing with frustrated desire.'

'But not for you, not for you,' she cried. 'I've learned that physical desire isn't everything and that there has to be more to a relationship. There has to be respect and trust between two people, as ... as there was between Andrew and me. He cared about me. But you don't and never did. You don't care what I'm thinking or feeling—if you did you wouldn't be here now. You'd respect my wishes and you'd leave instead of pestering me with amorous attentions that I can do very well without. . .'

'And have done without for some years, is my guess,' he jibed nastily, then added with a change of tone, his voice softening and deepening, 'But you don't have to any more. Remember that when you're lying awake at nights, lonely and frustrated.'

'Oh, go away. Go away!' Kathy whispered again, turning away from him into the room.

'I'll go, but I'll be back,' he told her. 'And maybe when I come again you'll have come round to my way of thinking. You can't wear the weeds of widowhood for ever, Kathy. You're too young, and they don't suit you. See you.'

Once again he left the house, leaving her struggling with chaotic emotions, standing alone in the sun-filled sitting room which she had worked so hard to make pretty and comfortable and which she felt expressed her own innate good taste in its colourings and furnishings.

But, since Lucas had set foot in it, it would never be the same. Even though he had gone his presence still lingered, powerful and exuding a sexuality that could neither be denied nor ignored. He had invaded her private space and had somehow defiled it. She would never be able to come into this room again without remembering what he had said to her and how he had kissed her. Arrogant as always, he had come and

taken something from her. And he would come
again, he had threatened. As long as she lived at
Seaview he would come.

'*Well, you can easily remedy that. Sell the
cottage and move out. Go back to Canada. You can
be sure I won't follow you there.*'

She remembered his angry suggestion that she
could always escape from his attentions by
ceasing to be his close neighbour as she sat down
at the desk in her bedroom and picked up paper
to slide into the typewriter.

Was that really what he wanted her to do? Was
he deliberately pestering her so that she would
sell the cottage, to him, of course, move out and
go away from Redcliffe? Had Mike been right
when he had suggested that Lucas would find
ways to trick her into leaving Seaview and selling
it to him?

She began to type, setting down the outline of
the plot of the next novel. As always, becoming
immersed in writing, she forgot about the passage
of time, Lucas and personal problems, and it was
almost midnight when she eventually stopped,
changed into her nightdress and dressing gown
and went down to the kitchen to make herself a
bedtime drink.

She had just put the catch on the Yale lock on
the back door and was going to put off the light
and go upstairs when she thought she heard a
noise in the back garden, and going over to the
small back window, she looked out. It was a clear
night and stars twinkled in the blue-black sky but
she couldn't see anyone in the shadowed garden.

Then she heard the noise again—a creaking

sound like the unoiled hinges of a door. The door of the garden shed? She went over to the dresser, pulled open a drawer and took out a flashlight she had put there for emergencies. Closing the drawer, she went to the back door, turned the knob on the Yale lock and quietly pulled the door open.

Outside it was cool and rather windy. The door on the garden shed creaked again, yet she was sure the door had been closed properly. She flicked on the torch, and its yellow beam swept over the shed. She walked across the grass, closed the door and shot the bolt on the front of it home. So much for thinking that Mrs Whelan's ghosts were haunting the place! she thought with a grin—and at that moment she heard the back door slam shut behind her.

Whirling round, she saw two dark figures racing for the pathway through the shrubbery.

'Hey, stop!' she shouted, and ran after them, holding up the skirt of her dressing gown so that she wouldn't trip over it, the beam from the torch wavering in front of her, lighting up trees and grass. Bushes snatched at her clothing and small stones pricked through the thin soles of her slippers.

She burst out of the bushes and on to the sweeping lawn at the side of Rowans. Yellow light spilled out of a wide patio window on that side of the house and she saw the two figures running across the illuminated grass.

'Stop! Come back!' she yelled, and set off in pursuit as they disappeared into the shadows at the corner of the house on their way to the front door, she guessed, remembering Mike's story about Keith the drummer seeing two figures going into Lucas's house.

Breathlessly she arrived on the gravel driveway at the front of Rowans. The wind whispered in the rowan trees and the stars sparkled in the sky. There were no dark figures on the steps leading up to the front door, and Kathy assumed they had gone into the house.

It was at this point that Keith the drummer had given up and had returned to Seaview. Mr Whelan, too, hadn't followed the figures all the way. But Kathy was made of sterner stuff. She was prepared to beard Lucas in his den and demand to know where the two persons she had seen trespassing on her property had gone and to accuse him of giving them sanctuary.

Switching off the torch, she marched determinedly up the steps to the front door.

CHAPTER FOUR

SHE was just raising her hand for a second time to the brass knocker on the door when the light over the doorway went on and the door swung back. Lucas stood there, tall and lean and somewhat forbidding. He was differently dressed from when he had called at her house, having changed his light suit for dark jeans and a dark jersey, as if he had been sailing. His black hair was ruffled, his chin was blurred by dark stubble and his eyes were heavy-lidded. Kathy thought he looked somewhat dissipated.

When he saw her his eyes widened slightly and he muttered a name. It sounded like 'Mary'. Then he frowned, passed a hand across his eyes as if he couldn't believe what he could see and expected her not to be there when he looked again.

'Where are they?' she demanded.

'Who?' His hand dropped to his side. He didn't look quite so sleepy now. His mouth curved downward at one corner and the line of cynicism running from his nose to his mouth deepened. 'Changed your mind, have you?' he jeered, his glance roving over her dressing gown, the lapels of which had fallen open to reveal the low cut of her nightgown. 'I see you've come suitably dressed for the occasion.'

It took a moment for her to absorb what he was saying, but then the implication behind his words became clear to her. *He thought she had come to sleep with him!*

She could think of no verbal retaliation, so she launched herself forward intending to slap his face, but she tripped over the doorstep and fell forwards instead. She landed against his chest and all the breath was knocked out of her. Lucas's arms closed about her instinctively as he rocked on his feet under the onslaught of her full weight. Instead of slapping him she reached up one hand to claw at his cheek. Cursing, he shoved her away from him, and she staggered a little too.

'What the hell was that for?' he rapped at her, the back of his hand against his cheek, his eyes glaring murderously at her.

'Take it back!' she fumed, pulling her gown about her so that she was properly covered up and tightening the belt about her waist. 'Take back what you just said and implied. Apologise for it. I haven't changed my mind about you. I'm not the sort of woman who goes about in the middle of the night looking for a man to sleep with, either. Take it back!'

'Then why are you here in the middle of the night dressed in your nightie?' he growled at her.

'I followed those two figures here.'

'What two figures?'

'The two people who were in my garden. They ran this way and I saw them come round to the front of the house.' Kathy realised that in his dark clothing Lucas could have been one of the figures she had seen. 'You could have been one of them.'

A hand to his forehead, he stared at her, still

frowning as if he was having trouble in taking in what she had said. Then he drawled mockingly,

'Now don't tell me you've been seeing ghosts like the Whelans!'

'They weren't ghosts. They were real,' she insisted. 'And they came this way. They came into this house, just like Keith—the drummer—said they did. He saw them too when he was living at the cottage and he followed them. Mike told me.'

'Oh, did he?' said Lucas drily. 'And you of course believed him because he's Andrew's cousin.'

'I might have known you'd cover up for them,' she sighed, feeling suddenly weak and helpless, as if she had come up against a hard, rock-like wall. 'But you're not going to get away with it any longer. Tomorrow I'm going to the police to tell them what I saw tonight. I'm going to tell them I followed two men here who could be smugglers and that you denied having seen them.'

'You're hysterical,' he jeered.

'I'm not. I never have hysterics.'

'Upset, then,' he went on diplomatically. 'It gave you a shock seeing figures in the garden.' He stepped round her and closed the front door. 'I think you'd better come in and we'll talk about this more calmly. I'd like to know where you got this idea that the people you saw could be smugglers and that I have something to do with them.'

A hand under her elbow, he urged her towards an archway on the right and into a wide long room furnished in contemporary style with big well-padded chairs and sofa. It was lit by two standard lamps, and from a hi-fi built into shelves on one side of the fireplace came the sound of music. On a coffee table in front of the armchairs was a whisky bottle and a half-full glass.

As soon as Lucas let go of her elbow Kathy turned back towards the archway.

'I must go back to the cottage,' she muttered.

'Later.' He side-stepped in front of her. 'You're not going until you've told me why you suspect me of having anything to do with smugglers. Sit down.'

She hesitated, judging her chances of getting past him and running out into the hall and from the house.

'Don't try,' he warned her. 'You'll get more than you bargained for if you do. Come on, now sit down and we'll talk. Would you like a drink?'

'No, thanks.' Kathy sat down rather sullenly on a chair opposite the one where he had obviously been sitting.

'It will help you relax, perhaps calm your nerves a little,' he suggested, sitting down. He had brought a second glass from a cabinet and now began to pour liqour into it.

'I'm not nervous,' she retorted, watching him pour more whisky into the half-full glass. 'Don't you think you've had enough?' she went on, realising that his ruffled appearance could be due to him having drunk too much whisky.

'Perhaps?' His smile came and went, mocking himself. 'Going to preach a sermon at me for drowning my sorrows? Here, take this, then I won't be drinking alone any more.' He handed the other glass to her and after a moment of reluctance she took it. She was feeling a little shaky now, reaction to the shock of seeing the two figures and then running after them setting in.

She sipped some of the drink, then sat back in the chair.

'Where are they, those two men?' she asked. 'You've hidden them, haven't you? They're somewhere in this house. You told them to hide when you heard me knocking at the door. That's why you were so long coming to answer the door, isn't it? You were telling them where to hide.'

He took a quick gulp of whisky, set his glass down and gave her a scathing glance.

'I took a long time to come to the door because I was half asleep when you knocked the first time and wasn't sure I had heard a knock,' he replied.

'But you weren't in bed. You're fully dressed. You hadn't gone to bed. You were sitting here drinking waiting for them to come, to bring their smuggled goods to you.' Kathy sipped more whisky. It was good, a little fiery, but warming, and it was easing her nerves a little. 'You were expecting someone when you opened the door,' she went on challengingly. 'Someone called Mary? Perhaps I didn't see two men. Perhaps one of them was a woman called Mary.'

'Ha!' His laugh was scornful as he flung himself back in his chair. In the shadows his eyes glittered at her. 'It's quite amazing,' he mocked.

'What is?'

'Your imagination, and your ability to invent a

ridiculous story about me receiving smugglers
here. I don't know any smuggers, and even if I
did I'd have nothing to do with them. No one
is in this house except me ... and now you.'
He leaned forward, elbows on his knees, his
dark eyes dancing suddenly with amusement.
'You've made it up, haven't you, this story
about seeing two people running to this house?
It's an excuse for you to come here after
midnight to see me.'

'Such conceit!' she retorted. 'Why would I
want to come and see you?'

'Because you're lonely and need a lover.'

'Oh, really, are you on about that again?' she
taunted, and putting down her glass got to her
feet. 'If that's all you can think about I'd better
go. I haven't made up a story as an excuse to
come and see you, and tomorrow I'm going to the
police to report that I saw two persons
trespassing on my property tonight. And I shall
tell them too of my suspicions concerning you!'

'*God!*' Lucas ground the oath out through set
teeth and he was there before her again, barring
the way. Taking hold of her upper arms, he
shook her slightly. 'What is it with you?' he
demanded roughly. 'Why are you so determined
to believe the worst of me? What have I ever
done to you, to deserve such treatment?'

'If you don't know, if you can't remember, it
isn't for me to say,' Kathy hissed.

'That's a bloody stupid remark to make,' he
jeered. 'I don't know, and I don't remember. So
you'll have to tell me.' He paused, his grasp of
her arms relaxing, his face changing, the

harshness fading. 'Tell me, Kathy, and I'll try to make amends,' he murmured, and with a half-stifled groan he put his arms around her and pulled her against him. 'Ah, Kathy, don't let's fight any more. If you knew how much I want you. . .'

'No. No!' She stepped back from him and looked up at him. It was a mistake, because he was very close to her and his eyes were smouldering with desire. 'No, Lucas,' she whispered desperately, 'please don't kiss me.'

'Why not? You know you're longing to be kissed,' he scoffed softly.

'Because . . . because I'm not ready yet.' Hands on his shoulders, she tried to push him away as he advanced again. 'It isn't long since Andrew died and I'm not ready to make love.'

'You'll be ready when I've finished with you,' he predicted confidently.

His fingertips slid over the pulse that was beating madly at the base of her throat and then along the collarbone, gently titillating the sensitive skin until every nerve was taut with a tingling awareness and her whole body quivered with delight when his lips tantalised the corner of her mouth before drifting lightly and insinuatingly along her jaw to the tender lobe of her ear. Closing her eyes, she fought to control the treacherous impulses surging through her, inciting her to give in to the desire he was arousing by his knowledgeable touch. But she fought a losing battle, and slowly the frigid tension in her body melted and her lips parted to his kiss. Her hands went up to caress his face, his hair, and for a few moments she was lost, drowning in a flood of delicious sensations.

'Not ready, did I hear you say?' he whispered against her cheek. 'Seems to me you're more than ready. Stay the night, Kathy. Stay and sleep with me.'

'No, no, I don't want to. I don't want to!' She struggled to free herself from his arms.

'We're both adults,' he argued, taking hold of her hands and removing them from his shoulders, holding them behind her back so that she was trapped again. 'And what we do privately can concern no one else. We have no other commitments and we have the opportunity, living next door to one another as we do and able to visit each other without anyone in the village knowing or seeing us, so you needn't worry about your reputation. We could both have a lot of pleasure, and it would be better for you than writing novels, better for me than sailing alone or drinking too much.'

His mouth swooped to hers again, and more than tempted by his softly spoken suggestion, Kathy made no attempt to resist, acknowledging the truth of what he had said. She was lonely and in need of any comfort he had to offer, and she could feel, by the way his hands were stroking her and moulding her body to his, his great need for comfort too.

Sensing her response, Lucas becan to kiss her more demandingly, his lips exploring her face roughly, his hands slipping within the opening of her robe. Groaning with pleasure at the sensations he was arousing, Kathy slid her hands under his jersey to caress the muscle-padded smoothness of his skin and to tantalise the hollows in his spine. Then unexpectedly something seemed to go *ping* in her mind, like the bell on a timer, warning her to go no further.

He could be making love to her deliberately to distract her while the men she had followed to his house made their getaway!

It was hard to assert mind over matter, to dominate physical desire with her will, but she did, and was pleased with herself for having the strength to do it. Pulling away from him, she folded her robe about her again as if it were a coat of armour she was putting on to protect herself from his attack.

'Now what's the matter?' demanded Lucas, raking his hair with one hand, and she felt her legs shake and her will falter when she saw how he was looking at her.

'How do I know you're not trying to distract me?' she whispered.

'Distract you from what?' He reached for her again, taking hold of her waist and jerking her forward until her breasts were brushed against his chest. Holding her there, he looked down at her, the expression on his face half tender, half lustful.

'From hearing those men leave,' Kathy gasped, clawing at his hands where they rested on her waist, scratching at them until he released her with a whispered curse. 'I saw them come here, I know I did. I didn't make it up as an excuse to come and see you.'

'All right, all right, I believe you. But you've got to believe me in return. I'm not making love to you to distract you. I'm making love to you because I want you.' He stepped towards her again but didn't touch her. 'Stop fighting me, Kathy—and stop fighting yourself too. You'll only get hurt if you go on fighting your instincts. This was bound to happen between us sooner or later. Might as well let it be now, preferably in my bed.'

'No. I must go back to the cottage. I . . . I can't do what you ask, Lucas. I can't have an affair with you, meeting secretly and then pretending when we meet in public that we're merely neighbours. I'm not like that. I'm going now. Please don't try to stop me again or force me to do anything against my will.'

Lucas stiffened at that, his face hardening again, his eyes narrowing.

'I don't go in for rape,' he retorted. His glance slid over her slowly and insolently and the corner of his mouth lifted in a slight mocking smile. 'And I don't believe it would be necessary in your case,' he drawled. 'But go on, leave if you want to. There'll be other times for you and me to be together.'

'Not if I can help it,' Kathy sniped shakily, and whirling round hurried from the room. In the hallway she found her torch on the table, picked it up and let herself out of the front door.

The stars were still bright, but the wind had died down. Across the lawn and along the pathway to the bushes she followed the beam of the torch to the back door of the cottage. As her fingers touched the doorknob she remembered suddenly that the catch of the Yale lock might still have been in place when the door had slammed shut, but she turned the knob just the same and tried to push the door open. It didn't budge. The catch had been in place and now she couldn't get into the kitchen.

The front door, of course. Walking round the side of the cottage, she tried to remember if she had turned the big key lock from the inside before she had gone up to type in her room. She was perhaps a little over-cautious about locking doors ever since the house she and Andrew had owned had been broken into one day when one of them had left a door unlocked for the other to get in. She turned the knob of the front door and pushed. It remained shut also. She was locked out of the cottage.

She knew that none of the downstairs windows were open, because she had closed them and locked them too. Only her bedroom window was open, the light shining out from it, and she couldn't reach that unless she had a step-ladder.

Where could she borrow a ladder? She knew there wasn't one in the garden shed. Who would have one? Lucas? Dared she go back and knock at his door and ask for his help? She could imagine the sardonic expression on his face when he saw her again tonight. He would think she had changed her mind about sleeping with him.

Yet where else could she go? She didn't want to stay out for the rest of the night. She supposed she could walk to the hotel and disturb the Travises, but then she would have to explain about chasing the figures across the lawn to Lucas's house, and they might wonder why she hadn't asked him for help.

Well, she had to make up her mind one way or the other; she couldn't stand there any longer growing colder. Back through the bushes, along the pathway to the lawn at the side of Rowans. No light streamed out from the living room across the grass, but there was a softer glow from a window on the same level on the same side of the house and she guessed he had gone into a bedroom.

The light over the front door was out, but the beam from her torch slid over the shape of his car which was parked casually in front of the garage door.

Perhaps there was a ladder in the garage, and if by any chance the garage door was unlocked she would be able to take the ladder out without disturbing him and carry it back to the cottage. It was worth a try.

The garage door was the overhead type. Kathy bent down to the handle near the bottom, took hold of it and pulled. To her relief the door came up quietly, moving on well-oiled rollers, and it slid back into the roof of the garage. Stepping inside, she shone the torch around. There were shelves around the walls holding cans of paint and car-cleaning materials. Garden tools hung neatly in a row from hooks.

She shone the torch upwards. As she had hoped, there was a rack built under the roof over which the door had slid. It seemed to be a storage place for boating equipment—and also for an aluminium extending ladder. Kathy resisted a desire to clap her hands and crow for pleasure when she saw it. Now all she had to do was lift it down, if she could reach it. She stretched an arm up. The end of the ladder was just beyond her reach.

She shone the torch around the garage again, searching for something on which she could stand. In a far corner there was a wooden crate, the sort in which bottles are packed. Going over to it, she dragged it to the place where the ladder jutted out from the overhead rack. She put her torch on a shelf so that it would shine upwards, then she climbed on to the crate. Stretching one arm upwards, she found she was able to grasp the end of the ladder.

. After several tugs, when it didn't move, she came to the conclusion that something heavy must be resting on it and preventing it from moving, so she pulled harder. It moved a little and she rested for a moment, drew a deep breath and calling on all her strength pulled again. The ladder began to slide towards her. She leaned backwards to take the weight of it as it came and, forgetting she was standing on the crate, she lost her balance, fell backwards to the floor. The ladder rushed on past her, falling with what seemed to her a deafening clatter to the floor, and missing her by inches.

Feeling bruised as she lay on the floor, Kathy didn't know whether to laugh or cry. Then she realised that the garage was attached to the house and Lucas might have heard the noise. He might come looking to find out who was in the garage, and before he did she must get out with the ladder, if possible.

She stood up and bent to lift the ladder,

thinking to carry it over one shoulder as she had seen men carrying ladders. But it was much heavier than she had expected and although she managed to lift it from the floor she had to let it down quickly, afraid she might damage herself internally if she persisted in lifting it.

Suddenly light flooded the garage and she turned defensively in the direction of a door, in the side of the garage, that communicated with the house. The door was open and Lucas stood there. He was dressed only in his jeans and the skin of his upper body gleamed in the electric light.

'What the hell are you doing?' he demanded, and stepped down into the garage. He strode towards her.

'I'm borrowing your ladder—at least, I'm trying to borrow it,' Kathy replied as calmly as she could, as if it was an everyday occurrence for a woman to creep, at dead of night, into her neighbour's garage to borrow his ladder. 'You see, I'm locked out of the cottage and the only way I can get in is through the bedroom window. I thought you'd gone to bed and I didn't want to disturb you again, so I just thought I'd borrow your ladder...' Her voice faltered slightly, because he looked so threatening with his dark eyebrows slanting into a frown and his lips compressed into a straight stern line. His bare forearms were very sinewy, she thought, and covered with black hairs, and the way he had folded his arms across his chest made the bicep muscles in his upper arms bulge.

'Go on,' he prompted, voice as soft as silk.

'Well, I fell off the crate and the ladder fell too. I'm sorry about the noise.' Kathy glanced warily at him, licked her dry lips and hurried on. 'Would you ... I mean, do you think you could carry the ladder to the cottage for me, put it up to the window and hold it while I climb up and get into the bedroom?' she ventured.

He didn't answer immediately but continued to stare at her from under frowning eyebrows.

'Lucas!' Her temper flared up suddenly. 'Answer me! I'm locked out and I don't want to spend the night outside. If you've any decency or any chivalry at all you'll help me.'

'But I've never claimed to be chivalrous. I don't happen to be a knight errant in one of your historical romances,' he jeered. 'I've always believed in the equality of the sexes. You're welcome to the ladder. I'm going back to bed. Good night!'

Turning on his heel, he began to stride back to the door through which he had come. Kathy followed him, furious because he was unwilling to help her.

'But I can't lift the ladder. It's too heavy for me,' she complained.

'Well, that's a pity, isn't it?' he drawled, turning to face her. 'You'll have to leave it where it is and find another way of getting into the cottage, won't you? Unless. . .' he paused to give her a glinting sidelong glance. 'Unless you'd like to spend the night with me. The offer I made earlier is still open.'

She was unprepared for the sudden leaping of her pulses. A garage smelling of petrol fumes and paint and lit by bright electric light is hardly the most romantic of places, but she was aware of a melting of her resistance to him again. Even though he had jeered at her and had refused to help her, the thought of being held in his arms again, of being able to rest her head on his shoulder and give in to the exciting caresses of his lips and hands, was overwhelming. Yet still she held back.

'Do you have a spare bedroom?' she asked.

'I do.'

'Then I'll stay for the rest of the night and perhaps in the morning you'll help me to get into the cottage.'

'It's a deal,' said Lucas cryptically, and turned towards the door again.

'As long as you don't think that I came back to borrow the ladder just as an excuse to see you again,' she said, following him.

'Does it really matter to you what I think about you?' he challenged, stopping suddenly and swinging round to face her.

'Yes, I suppose it does,' she admitted. 'I don't want you thinking I would go out of my way to ... to...'

'Seduce me?' he suggested softly, standing close to her. 'Oh, you've already done that tonight, just by coming to my house ... twice. But it's cool standing out here. Come in.'

They stepped into a big kitchen, all shining formica surfaces, stainless steel, mellow wood panelling with a glint of copper pans, and crossed it to another doorway into the hallway which was in darkness. From the far end of the passage came the glow of light.

'I'd like to wash my hands,' said Kathy.

'There's a bathroom here.' Lucas pushed open a door, flicked on a light. 'Help yourself.'

The bathroom was large and luxurious with a deep bath sunk into the floor, gleaming tiles and mirrors. Kathy washed her hands and her face, which was streaked with dirt, then surveyed herself critically in one of the mirrors. She was surprised to see how serene she looked, her hair shining, her face glowing from the wash. It was true there was some dirt on her dressing gown, but on the whole she looked remarkably cool and elegant, in spite of her adventure with the ladder.

She left the bathroom, switching off the light, and immediately found herself in darkness in the hallway. The only light came from the room at the end of the passage.

'Lucas?' she called.

'In here.' His voice came from where the light glowed, so she wandered in that direction and stepped through a doorway into a wide room with two picture windows covered with rust-coloured curtains. The carpet was cream and the bed was a wide low divan also covered with rust-coloured linen. The chests of drawers were made of teak.

'Is this the spare bedroom?' asked Kathy. Lucas was by a bedside table setting a radio alarm clock.

'No, it's mine,' he replied. He put down the radio clock and came towards her. 'Are you all right? Did you hurt yourself when you fell in the garage?'

His sudden concern about her had the effect of softening her attitude towards him.

'No, not much. I'm lucky the ladder didn't fall on me though,' she said.

'You were foolish to try and get it down yourself,' he told her. 'But then you were always the same, determined to do everything yourself, independent to the nth degree. That's something else about you that hasn't changed, like your eyes. And your hair.' He came close and raised a hand to touch her hair gently, lifting his fingers through its silkiness.

'The spare bedroom,' Kathy muttered shakily. The hot weakness was flooding through her and she longed to touch him too, to stroke the crisp hairs that criss-crossed his chest.

'The beds aren't made up in there,' he said, still playing with her hair. 'You can sleep in here.'

'And you?' She couldn't look at him. Her glance seemed to be riveted on the strong column of his throat. 'Where will you sleep?'

'With you. And not for the first time.'

His arms went around her and his lips claimed hers again. She didn't try this time to subdue the desire to be with him that surged through her. All the love she had felt for him nine years ago burst out of the depths where it had been stored away, unknown to her, and overcame the defences she had built up over the years to protect herself from it.

His fingers, seeking and finding what gave her most pleasure, were gentle at first, as were his lips, but gradually as his passion blazed he became more ruthless and demanding, arousing in her a desperate aching need that had to be satisfied. In her turn she became demanding too, twisting and turning against him as they lay across the bed, kissing him wherever she could, pinching and stroking him until both of them, carried beyond all reason, beyond their immediate surroundings, soared up together to a wonderful explosive climax and, united at last, they seemed to melt into each other.

And for Kathy it was like coming home at last to a warm fire after being lost in a cold wasteland for many years.

She was wakened the next morning by the alarm clock bell pealing softly, followed by gentle music. Starting up in the bed, she looked around the strange sunlit room and remembered what had happened. Cautiously she glanced sideways. Lucas was beside her, lying on his stomach, the skin of his broad bare shoulders glowing with a copper tone in the morning sunshine against the pale yellow sheets, his hair a tangled black mop against the pillow. He didn't seem to have heard the alarm clock.

Slowly Kathy lay back and pulled the sheet up over her, thinking back to the wild abandonment of their lovemaking and feeling a strange stirring of shame because after all she had been no better than he, taking what she had wanted from him without a thought as to the consequences of their act of love.

The alarm clock rang again and Lucas reached out an arm to turn it off. He heaved over on to his back with a sigh and opened his eyes. He blinked several times, frowned, then turned his head to look at her. Slowly he smiled, an intimate knowledgeable smile.

'So you're still here,' he murmured.

'Yes, but I shouldn't be. I'd like to go to the cottage now. Please will you carry the ladder over there and help me to get in?'

'Now? Immediately?' He frowned again.

'Yes, now.'

Supporting himself on one elbow, Lucas leaned over her.

'Won't you stay to breakfast?' he asked, beginning to play with her hair, his dark eyes glancing warmly at her lips.

'No, I can't stay any longer. I must go. Please will you do as I ask,' she said, pulling her hair from his grasp and shifting away from him almost frantically, afraid that he might overwhelm her again with his lovemaking. 'You promised you would if I stayed the night with you.'

'All right, I'll help you get into the cottage if you'll make another promise to go sailing with me this weekend,' he agreed. 'I have some business in town this morning and this afternoon, but I'll be back around four o'clock. We could leave after high tide, go along the coast. . .'

'Oh, I should have guessed you'd want more!' Kathy exclaimed, resisting with all her might. She covered her eyes with her hands, shutting out the tempting sight of him. 'Oh, I wish I'd never come here last night! I wish I'd gone to someone else for help. I should have known I'd have to pay in some way for your help.'

There was a bleak little silence, then she heard him draw in a harsh breath.

'It works both ways, as I see it,' he said coldly. 'I gave you something, too, last night—I didn't do all the taking. But since you seem to have regrets this morning about what we did we'll leave it there. I'll take the ladder over to Seaview and climb up to the bedroom. The back door should be open by the time you get there.'

He moved away from her and off the bed. Between her spread fingers she saw him pull on his clothes. He left the room and she sat for a while, her hands sliding down her cheeks, tears welling briefly in her eyes as she realised how much it had hurt her to rebuff him.

By the time she left the bedroom to go to the bathroom Lucas had gone from the house. A few minutes later Kathy left too. The grass of the lawn was damp with dew and morning mist drifted above the river estuary. When she reached her own garden Lucas was coming across to the pathway, the ladder over one shoulder. Behind him the back door of the cottage was wide open.

'Thank you,' she whispered, unable to face the cold contemptuous glance he gave her.

'Next time don't leave home without your back door key,' he retorted sardonically. 'About going sailing this afternoon. . .'

'I . . . I'll let you know,' she said hurriedly. 'I . . . I can't tell you now.'

'If you decide to come be at the jetty at four,' he said brusquely, and strode away along the path.

Once she was in the house Kathy went straight up to her bedroom. From the dressing table Andrew's brown eyes gazed at her from his photograph, not accusingly, but with a certain smile hiding the sadness, and she groaned in an agony of shame.

What had she done? And why had she done it? She picked up the photograph and studied it. Andrew hadn't been handsome or distinguished-looking as Lucas was, but he hadn't been unpleasant to look at, and there had always been a smile lurking in his eyes. Hiding the sadness. Or the knowledge, perhaps, that he knew he was going to die young? Or the knowledge that his wife hadn't loved him the way he might have wanted to be loved? As if he had known she loved another man more passionately than she had loved him. As if he had known about her brief passionate first love-affair with Lucas.

Had Andrew guessed she had found it difficult to make love with him? Had he sensed she had always been comparing his lovemaking with that of another man? Oh, she hoped not. She sincerely hoped not. Not for anything would she have hurt him in such a way.

And now she was feeling guilty because last night she had given in to Lucas and had gone along the path of sensuous pleasure with him, a path he knew so well and to which he was such an expert guide. How many other women had he tempted with passion? Mary? Jane Mortimer Smith? And there must have been other fish to fry over the years.

Last night the floodtide of temptation had swept over her and she had let herself drown in it. But this morning the tide was out. Her head was clear and Lucas wasn't anywhere near her. Now she could see how it would be if she did what he had suggested. They would have an affair, two adults meeting privately when they felt a mutual desire to meet, satisfying each other's sexual needs but otherwise staying aloof from each other. There would be no emotional involvement, no commitment.

'It's no use, Andy,' she said to the photograph. 'I can't do it. I'm not made that way. If he can't make any commitment to me I can't do it. I can't sleep with him any old time he wants me to. Last night—well, last night was what you might call an aberration, a temporary lapse. You see, I . . . I've been so lonely these past months since you died. But it won't happen again. Next time. . .'

Realising she was talking to herself, she broke off and shook her head. There wasn't going to be a next time with Lucas, if she could avoid it. She wouldn't go to his house any more and she wouldn't let herself be alone with him ever again. She wouldn't go sailing with him today, because if she did he would only take her to some secluded place where he would make love to her.

But she had to do something. She couldn't stay in the house all day moping and feeling guilty. She would go out. She would drive to Castle Douglas, call in at Mike's shop and look at record-players, and after choosing one she would drive on to Glen Trool in the mountains of Galloway to take photographs of the historic site as part of the research for her next novel. Lucas could go sailing, as he often did, by himself.

CHAPTER FIVE

IT was almost noon when Kathy drove down the main street of Castle Douglas and turned into a side street to park her car. She found Mike's shop on the sunny side of the main street and stepped inside. There were several people there browsing over the wide selection of records and tapes, and one couple were being shown the advantages of a certain TV which was advertised as being the bargain of the week.

A youngish man in jeans and checked shirt who was wearing a headband around his long fair hair approached her and asked if he could help her. When she turned to face him fully he drew back a step and his large grey, rather watery-looking eyes literally goggled at her as if he were astonished to see her.

'I'd like to see Mike Austin. Is he in?' asked Kathy, suppressing a desire to ask him if he had seen a ghost or if there was something horrific about her appearance.

'Er ... yes. He's ... he's in the office ... on the phone,' he muttered, backing away from her. 'I'll tell him you're here.'

Turning quickly, he almost ran through a doorway at the back of the shop. Kathy turned away to examine the stereo equipment set out on shelves behind her, her foot beating time to the music that was blaring forth from some loud-speakers.

'Kathy! It's great to see you again. I was wondering when you'd be popping in.' Speaking just behind her, Mike sounded welcoming, and she turned to smile at him. 'You've come to look at some hi-fis?'

'Yes. Now what can you show me?'

'Plenty.' His grin was cheerful and there was a glimmer of admiration in his hazel eyes as their glance swept over her. He seemed genuinely pleased to see her, and that did a lot for her morale. 'I'm glad you've turned up,' he went on. 'How about having lunch with me after I've shown you a few record players? We can go to the Italian place around the corner?'

'Sounds like a good idea,' she said enthusiastically.

For the next half hour or so Mike showed off his best sales technique as he presented various makes of turntables, amplifiers and speakers to her, pointing out their advantages and disadvantages and quoting prices, until Kathy felt quite dizzy and had to ask him to stop while she absorbed the information and was able to make a decision.

'You have so many different makes,' she remarked.

'We pride ourselves on having the best selection in the south of Scotland, perhaps in the whole of Scotland,' he told her with a grin. 'There isn't any make of equipment you can't buy at Austin's. Shall we go to lunch now?'

He asked the young man with the headband to

keep an eye on the shop for a couple of hours, then ushered Kathy out of the shop, along the street and down a side street.

The restaurant, bright with red tablecloths, imitation brickwork and festooned with hanging baskets of fern-like plants, was called the Villa Romana, and the proprietors had obviously tried to re-create a Roman atmosphere in a Scottish country town. It was full of shoppers and tourists, but a table had been reserved for Mike.

'It's not long been open,' he explained as they sat down at the table for two near a window. 'The food is super, and although they specialise in Italian dishes I can really recommend the fish and chips. The fish is fresh every day. None of that frozen stuff!'

A waitress came to the table and took their orders, returning with a carafe of house wine, some hot bread in a basket and whipped butter in a dish. Mike poured wine into the glasses.

'So how did the move go?' he asked. 'Are you all settled in?'

'More or less.'

'Any neighbours called on you yet?'

'Only Lucas MacBride.'

He glanced at her sharply across the table.

'Really? Why would he do that? What did he want?'

'Oh, he was just being neighbourly,' shrugged Kathy, avoiding his eyes and wishing she hadn't mentioned Lucas. To her annoyance her cheeks grew warm as she recalled just how neighbourly she and Lucas had been during the past night. 'No harm in that, is there?' she challenged lightly.

'No, I suppose not,' agreed Mike. The waitress came with two bowls of salad, green lettuce, red tomatoes and crisp onion rings, and set them down. Mike helped himself to a chunk of the warm crusty bread and buttered it liberally. 'It might be a good idea for you to steer clear of MacBride, though,' he commented, and took a bite of the bread.

'Why?'

He chewed for a few seconds before answering, then leaned towards her across the table, his eyes dark and intent.

'As you're a newcomer to Redcliffe everything you do is going to be watched very closely and talked about.'

'Gossiped about, you mean, don't you?' Kathy said drily. 'Oh, I know that. And it doesn't just happen in Redcliffe. It happens everywhere.'

'And doesn't it bother you?'

'Not really. You see, I'm not ashamed of anything I've done or am likely to do,' she replied, and this time her cheeks didn't grow warm as she returned his gaze. 'And I really don't see how passing the time of day with Lucas MacBride, my nearest neighbour, can give cause for gossip. After all, it must be known that he handled the transfer of ownership of Seaview Cottage to Andrew. He was my late husband's lawyer over here, so he and I are likely to have some valid reason for talking to each other.'

'I realise that,' said Mike, nodding his head. 'Passing the time of day with your nearest neighbour or with someone you've done business with shouldn't give rise to gossip. But in this case the problem lies with this particular neighbour. MacBride has a bad reputation.'

'As a lawyer, you mean?'

'Well, I have heard that he's not above making a quick quid out of his clients if he can. Same with the property deals he handles.' The waitress came with two plates piled high with golden chips, fish in crisp batter and bright green peas. She set them down and went away. 'Actually, I was referring not to his reputation as a lawyer,' continued Mike, speaking again in that low serious tone he adopted when he wanted to convince Kathy that he was speaking the truth. 'I was referring to his reputation with women.'

'Oh.' Kathy declined the ketchup he had offered her and watched him shake some of the thick red sauce on to the edge of his plate. Amusement bubbled up inside her suddenly. 'Now you've intrigued me,' she said, mocking him a little. 'One sure way of making a woman more than ever interested in a man is to refer to his reputation with women. You mean, I suppose, that Lucas MacBride is a rake, to use an old-fashioned term for a womaniser.'

'That's as good a description as any,' said Mike, still serious. 'I mean that he's had more than one affair with a local woman since he came to live in Redcliffe.'

'With whom, for instance?' challenged Kathy as she spiked a long chip with her fork.

'Well, I can't give you any names,' said Mike vaguely.

'Would Jane Mortimer Smith be one of them?' she asked, pinning him down.

'Yes, as a matter of fact she is the most constant member of his harem,' Mike said maliciously. 'How's your fish?'

'Delicious.'

'And then there are some who say that he has a wife stashed away somewhere in a loony bin,' he added. He seemed to be relishing the gossip he was passing on to her almost as much as the food he was eating.

'Don't you mean a hospital for the treatment of mental illness?' said Kathy sternly, suddenly disliking his casual malice.

'I suppose I do.' His grin was cheeky and unrepentant. 'Same thing.'

'Calling a hospital where people are treated for nervous breakdowns and other mental upsets a loony bin is ... is like calling an Italian a wop or a Frenchman a frog,' she rebuked him severely. 'Really, Mike, how can you be so prejudiced? People can't help becoming mentally ill, any more than they can help catching the common cold.'

'Sorry,' he apologised with a shrug. 'I didn't know you felt so strongly about such things. It's just a way of speaking, Kathy. I was using a term that's been around for a long time.' He grinned at her again.

'I do feel strongly. I think it's very sad that some people aren't equipped with the mental stamina to cope with the stress and strains of modern life and that they have to receive specialised treatment in a hospital,' she argued. 'And none of us should be in too much of a hurry to judge anyone who has to stay in such a hospital. Nor should we judge the behaviour of their next of kin too hastily. You know the saying, Mike: "There but for the grace of God. . ." '

'I know it,' he interrupted with impatience, his narrow face seeming to become narrower, his thin lips tightening viciously. 'But that doesn't alter my opinion of Lucas MacBride, and I think you'll agree he shouldn't be playing around with other women while his wife is in hospital.'

'But you said it was only hearsay that he has a wife. You said there are some who say,' objected Kathy, wondering if the fact that he had a wife suffering from a mental disease could be the reason why Lucas often looked so morose.

'Hearsay that she's in hospital somewhere,' corrected Mike smoothly. 'He had a wife when he came to live in Redcliffe—she was seen at his house. But she hasn't been seen around for the past three to four years.'

'Maybe she left him,' suggested Kathy.

'Maybe she did. Anyway, I thought you ought to be warned about being too friendly with him,' said Mike coolly. 'Now, let's change the subject, shall we?' He smiled at her. 'I wouldn't want a disagreement about Lucas MacBride to come between us. Have you decided which record player and hi-fi system you prefer?'

'Yes, I think I have,' said Kathy, only too glad to get away from the rather worrisome subject of Lucas's 'wife', and for the rest of the meal they discussed her choice and how she should pay for the equipment.

'I won't take it with me right now,' she decided

as they left the restaurant. 'I'm going to drive over to Glen Trool this afternoon.'

'Whatever for?' Mike seemed surprised.

'Oh, to look around. I'm interested in the battle that took place there and I'd like to have a look at the site and take a few photographs. It's part of the research for my next novel.'

'Well, I'll tell you what we'll do,' said Mike as they entered the shop. 'You pay for it on a credit card and I'll bring it to you tomorrow afternoon. That will save you having to come back here on your way back from Glen Trool. You see, we close early on Saturday afternoon. And then it would be best if I bring it to you and show you how to install it, or even do that for you. Is it okay with you if I come over about three tomorrow?'

'That will be fine. You'll stay for supper?' Kathy suggested.

'I'd like to,' he said, and they parted on good terms, although Kathy was conscious of a slight withdrawal on her part. Mike wasn't as like Andrew as she had first believed. He was more given to malicious remarks about other people than Andrew had been. There was a hard edge to him that grated a little on her sensitivity.

She enjoyed the drive through the sunlit green countryside to the pretty village of Gatehouse of Fleet and from there along the road that curved beside the glinting water of the estuary of the river Cree. From Newton Stewart she continued along the same riverside road until she reached the House of the Hill, where a narrow road turned off to the right. From that junction the hill road climbed steadily to a signpost with the words Glen Trool on it. Turning on to yet another narrow twisting road, she followed it beside the tumbling rock-strewn Water of Trool, passing plantations of dark conifers until she reached a stretch of open moorland where sheep cropped grass among scattered grey rocks and the wind sighed softly over the steep valley and a whaup cried forlornly.

There were other cars parked in the space provided and other people were walking about or picnicking as they admired the panoramic views of distant hills. On a huge boulder Kathy read an inscription. In the year 1306 Robert the Bruce and his followers had defeated a large number of their enemies by rolling rocks down the nearby cliff on to the men who had been climbing up to the top of it.

Kathy walked to the edge of the cliff and gazed downwards. Below, a small loch gleamed like a blue jewel caught in a dark setting of rocks and trees. She tried to imagine what it had felt like to have been one of the men who had rolled the rocks on to the other men, and failed. Such cunning, such violence belonged to another age of bitter enmity and strife when there had been little respect for the life of an individual, and no tolerance at all of differences in opinion and no freedom of choice for the ordinary person.

Instead she found herself thinking of Mike's intolerant remarks about Lucas. Had they been made out of spite because Lucas had evicted Mike and his friends from Seaview? Or had they been based on the truth? Was it true that Lucas had a wife who was mentally ill and in hospital somewhere? How could she find out if it were true or not? By asking Lucas, she supposed. But then would he tell her the truth?

'They really didn't stand a chance, did they?' An American-accented voice spoke beside her and she turned to find an elderly man standing there looking through the lens of his camera down the cliffside.

'No, they didn't. It must have been horrible for the men climbing up,' she said, slinging forward her own camera, a Canon F-1 that Andrew had given her for her last birthday.

'Light's pretty bright today for this country,' said the American. 'Not often it's as clear as this. Usually there's a lot of mist. We've just come down from Skye, and this area is a lot different from up there. The scenery is much softer, more rolling. Are you touring too?'

'No. I live quite near here.'

In no time they were discussing what lens to use and how to set their cameras for the best pictures of the views. The American introduced himself as Hiram B. Stewart and claimed to be descended from the Royal Stewarts and Robert the Bruce. Then he introduced her to his wife Amy who was sitting in their rented car, and Kathy spent a pleasant half hour talking with them. She left them after inviting them to call on her at Seaview if they should decide to drive down to Redcliffe and the coast.

To her surprise it was almost four o'clock, the time Lucas had suggested that she should meet him at the jetty if she decided to go sailing with him. Well, she wasn't going sailing with him, but perhaps she ought to tell him she wasn't going with him, and even though it was after five when she at last drove into Redcliffe she went straight to the jetty to see if he was still there waiting for her.

It looked as if a race had just started, because a group of dinghies, sails shining in the sunlight were all heeled over on the stiff breeze as they forged through the water down the estuary towards the sea.

Shading her eyes against the bright beams of the sun, Kathy looked over at the pool where Lucas's boat was usually moored. It was still there. He hadn't gone without her. Then where was he?

Turning away from the jetty, she walked up to the old grey house which was the yacht clubhouse and went in. A few people were lounging about one of the rooms, and she asked one of them if he had seen Lucas MacBride.

'He's away in the race,' was the answer.

So he hadn't waited for her. Kathy wasn't sure whether to feel relieved or piqued because he hadn't. Leaving the clubhouse, she glanced again at the racing dinghies, wondering which one Lucas was in, then deciding that they wouldn't be back for at least an hour and a half she climbed into her car and drove to the cottage.

To her surprise the gate was open, as if someone had been to the cottage and had neglected to close it when he or she had left, and she wondered if Lucas had called for her. She walked up to the front door, searching in her handbag for the key. She found it and took it out, looked up and straight at the door.

It wasn't closed.

Kathy stood and stared. Her heart missed a beat and began to race as she examined the slightly open door. It had been damaged, attacked with something like an axe, she imagined, around the area of the lock and then burst open.

Someone had broken into the cottage while she had been out. Was that someone still inside waiting to attack her when she went in?

Taking a deep breath and gathering all her courage together, she pushed the door wide—and gasped with outrage when she saw that the floor of the small entrance hall was flooded with water which was pouring through the bathroom doorway. Taking off her sandals, she waded through the tepid water under the curve of the stairway and into the bathroom. All the taps were open and water was gushing out of them. Both the hand-basin and the bathtub were filled to overflowing. Quickly she turned off the taps and looked around. The cupboard above the hand-basin had been torn from the wall and was in pieces on the floor, its mirror shattered, its contents strewn about.

Someone had broken into the cottage and vandalised it!

Dreading what she would find in the kitchen, Kathy waded through ankle-deep water into the kitchen. The water had spread across the floor, soaking the rugs she had put down on the newly painted stone floor. The new table and chair set had been broken up and splintered and torn wood was scattered about. The shelves of the dresser had been swept clear of the dishes she had arranged on them and the blue and white crockery lay smashed on the floor, together with the shattered glassware that had been taken from the dresser cupboards, the doors of which had been wrenched from their hinges.

Throbbing with anger and outrage, she went up the stairs—and could have screamed with fury when she saw what had been done to her bedroom. Curtains had been ripped down and torn to shreds. Bedclothes and mattress had been slashed with a knife. The typewriter had been destroyed completely and everything that had been on top of the dressing table had been swept to the floor and smashed. With a cry of distress she went over to pick up the photograph frame from the floor. It was twisted and empty. She found the photograph of Andrew nearby. It had been ripped into several pieces.

With the pieces in her hand she stood up. This destruction of her property, this vandalism done in broad daylight while she had been absent from the cottage, had been done deliberately by someone who had a grudge against her and who perhaps didn't want her to stay and live at Seaview.

Who? Lucas?

Because he didn't want her living in this house? Because as Mike had once suggested Lucas was the receiver of smuggled goods and was worried she might go to the police and tell them about the men she had seen last night running towards his house?

She looked around the room again as if she could find the answer to her questions among the debris; as if among her destroyed and damaged possessions she would find some clue that would help her discover the identity of the vandal.

No, Lucas could never do something like this. Whatever else he was, Lucas wasn't vindictive. If he wanted her to give up Seaview and go away from Redcliffe he would use much more subtle means.

Then who?

Placing the torn photograph on the dressing table, she left the room, went downstairs and outside. She put on her sandals, picked up her handbag and camera, pulled the broken door closed as far as she could and went down the pathway. It wasn't far to the nearest phone at the hotel, but she drove there and parked her car in front of the building.

But before phoning the police she decided to find Polly Travis to tell her what had happened and to get advice from her or Harry as to what she should do next. She had to tell someone what had happened; she couldn't keep this awful violation of her home and her possessions to herself much longer.

There were a few people in the lounge of the hotel. Guessing that Polly would be in the kitchen supervising the preparation of dinner, Kathy went right through to the public bar, hoping to find Harry there, but only a stranger was there, arranging bottles on the shelves at the back of the bar.

'Is Mrs Travis about?' she asked when the bartender asked her what she wanted.

'Not today,' he replied cheerfully. 'She and Harry have taken the day off to go and see her mother in the nursing home and to do some shopping. Anything I can do to help?'

'No—no, thanks,' she said quickly, hiding her disappointment. Leaving the bar, she went back into the lounge. Frustrated in her desire to confide in Polly, wondering where she was going to spend the night since she couldn't stay at the cottage, she hardly looked where she was going, and collided with a man who had just entered the hotel.

'Hey, watch out! You're going to come a cropper if you don't look where you're going,' said a pleasantly lilting Scottish voice, and Kathy looked up at a broad, suntanned face topped by a quiff of greying brown wavy hair, a face that was familiar but that she couldn't quite place yet.

'Well, I'll be darned! You're Kathy Warren, aren't you?' exclaimed the man, and laughed, showing big white teeth, his blue-grey eyes twinkling with good humour. He thrust out his right hand. 'Remember me?'

Putting her right hand in his to shake it, Kathy racked her memory, thinking back to the times she had stayed in Redcliffe years ago. There had been a young man, stockily built with a broad reddish face and a quiff of brown hair, who had been friendly with her friends Judi and Joan Young. He could easily have matured into this self-assured person who was smiling at her as if he were sincerely pleased to see her again.

'Kenny?' she ventured.

'Right first time. You know, when my wife

described you to me last night and said you'd worked at the hotel and had crewed for Lucas some years ago I wondered then if she was talking about you, but she called you Kathy Reid. Well, it's good to see you, Kathy. Come and have a drink.'

'Your wife?' she asked cautiously, going with him into the lounge.

'Jane. You were to tea with her yesterday afternoon I believe.'

'Oh. *You're* Dr Smith!' she exclaimed.

'Right.' He pulled out a chair for her at one of the round tables. 'What will you have?'

She chose a sweet Martini and he went to the bar to get the drinks. She watched him going, realising that she had never known his last name nor that he had been studying to be a doctor. He had just been Kenny, one of the crowd of young people at the yacht club. Oh, how long ago it all seemed, when she had been young and innocent, in love with life and in love with Lucas.

And now Kenny was Dr Kenneth Smith and married to Lady Jane, and she was Andrew Reid's widow who had just had her house vandalised and was . . . Her thought stumbled. She had been going to think, or had been going to say to herself, that she wasn't in love with Lucas any more, but the words wouldn't form in her mind because it wasn't true; because the truth of the matter was *she was still in love with Lucas*.

Kenny came back with the drinks and sat down at the table in such a position that he had a good view of the entrance and of anyone who might come into the lounge.

'Cheers,' he said, raising his glass tankard of beer and promptly drinking half of it. 'So you're living at Seaview Cottage.' His eyes twinkled knowingly. 'Nice and cosy for you and Lucas!'

About to raise her glass to her lips, Kathy gave him a sharp glance.

'What are you getting at?' she demanded.

'Oh, come on, Kathy, don't be coy,' he chided her. 'I know as well as you that you and Lucas had something going when you used to crew for him.'

'People change,' she said coolly. 'I've been married to someone else. Happily married.' She stressed the word 'happily'. 'And Lucas has. . .' She broke off and leaned towards him. 'Is Lucas married, Kenny?' she whispered.

'He has been,' he replied, much as Lucas had replied when she had asked him the same question. 'But I wouldn't let that come between you and him,' he continued lightly, almost flippantly. 'Do you ever see the Young girls these days?' he asked, nimbly changing the subject.

'No. I did write to Judi for a while from Canada, but then she married too and went off to live in Australia and I didn't hear from her any more. Joan I believe is living in London now. I saw Mrs Young when I was at my parents' home a few weeks ago. How long have you and Jane been married, Kenny?'

'Must be going on for three years,' he replied with a grin. 'She turned up in my surgery one day and swept me right off my feet.'

He continued to talk in a rambling sort of way

about his courtship of Jane and then of other people they had both known when they had stayed in Redcliffe nine years previously, and Kathy only half listened as she tussled with the problem of the vandalising of the cottage, wondering whether she should go and phone the police or wait until she had seen Lucas and let him handle the whole business as her lawyer.

'The race should be over now,' she became aware of Kenny saying. 'I wonder how Jane fared.'

'She's racing tonight?'

'If she could find someone to crew for her. Trevor, her regular crew, couldn't make it tonight, so she was hoping she could pick up a crew at the club,' said Kenny, watching the entrance. His face brightened suddenly. 'Ah, there's Lucas.' He stood up and waved and called out, 'Hey, Luke—over here!'

On his way through to the public bar, Lucas stopped in mid-stride and turned to look into the lounge. Slowly he came towards them. He was in sailing clothes and looked so vigorous and handsome that Kathy felt her heart jerk and the familiar heat of desire flood through her. Then as he drew near she saw the expression in his eyes as he looked at her. He looked as if he hated her.

'Sit down,' Kenny said hospitably. 'Remember Kathy? Have you seen Jane anywhere?'

'I've just left her in the yacht club,' said Lucas, but he didn't sit down. 'We won the race.'

'You crewed for her?' Kenny looked both gratified and surprised. 'Good. This calls for a celebration. Think I should order champagne?'

'You can do what the hell you like,' growled Lucas. 'I'm not staying.'

And without acknowledging that he had seen Kathy, let alone remembered her, he turned on his heel and walked out of the lounge.

'We ... ell!' exclaimed Kenny, looking completely perplexed. 'I wonder what's got into him? I hope Jane hasn't been behaving too officiously. She can be very bossy, you know, but she means well. And then Luke always was a moody devil. . .'

'Excuse me, Kenny,' Kathy got to her feet, 'I must catch him. I have to tell him something—it's about the cottage. Thanks for the drink. I'll see you again some time.'

Not waiting to hear his protests, she hurried from the lounge into the public bar to check that Lucas wasn't in there, and then not seeing him among the men leaning against the bar, she hurried back to the front entrance of the hotel, went out and looked around to see which way he had gone. At last she saw him, he was covering the ground quite fast as he strode along by the sea-wall in the direction of Rowans.

Flinging herself into her car, Kathy backed out of the parking space and drove after him. She passed him and drove on, swerving in between the open gates of Rowans to park beside his Jaguar. When Lucas came through the gateway she was standing beside her car waiting for him. He saw her and stopped.

'What do you want?' he demanded roughly.

'Something . . . something awful has happened,' she whispered, going right up to him. His eyes were as dark and glittery as jet as he stared down at her. 'While I was out today someone broke into the cottage and . . . and vandalised it. They've broken the furniture, thrown dirt at the walls and scribbled obscenities on them, left the taps open so that water flooded the place, slashed the bed, torn the curtains and . . . and torn up Andrew's photograph . . . the only decent one I had of him. Oh, it's awful! Awful!'

'Have you phoned the police?' he asked, his voice harsh.

'No, not yet. I didn't get home until after five, and when I saw what had been done I went straight over to tell Polly, but she wasn't there, and then I ran into Kenny and. . .'

'Polly? Why would you want to tell her?'

'Well, I felt I had to tell someone, and I couldn't find you,' she said defensively. 'Someone told me you'd gone racing when I went to the jetty to meet you as we'd arranged. Then Kenny asked me to have a drink with him and. . .' She became aware that with an expression of annoyance he had turned away from her and was striding towards the house. 'Oh, where are you going? What are you going to do? Aren't you going to help me?' she exclaimed, running after him.

Lucas paused halfway up the steps to the front door of the house and looked back at her. The expression on his face was grimly sardonic.

'Are you quite sure you want *my* help?' he challenged her coldly.

He wasn't a bit kind or loving as Andrew would have been in a similar situation. Andrew would have taken time to comfort her. He would have held her hand and spoken to her reassuringly. Lucas's behaviour was like a shower of ice-cold water, bracing and lacking in sentiment, but it stiffened her backbone, prevented her from wallowing in a flood of self-pity. She tossed back her head and glared up at him.

'I suppose I'll have to pay through the nose for it, but yes, I do want your help . . . as a lawyer, of course,' she retorted.

The hardness left his face. His eyes glimmered with amusement and his smile flickered in and out.

'In that case I can hardly refuse,' he drawled. 'Come into the house. I'll phone the police and ask them to come down and look at the cottage. They'll want a statement from you, will ask you a lot of questions about why you're living here and where you've been this afternoon. Will you be prepared to answer them?'

'Oh, yes, I'll tell them everything,' she replied, following him into the house. 'I'll tell them about the figures I saw last night too running across your lawn. Do you agree to me doing that?'

Standing by the phone in the living room, the receiver in his hand, Lucas gave her a sidelong glance and said thoughtfully,

'Yes, I agree to that. I'm sure they'll be interested.'

The police, a sergeant accompanied by a constable, lost no time in driving out to inspect the damage done at the cottage. They asked Kathy many questions and she answered them all truthfully, telling them about her visit to Castle Douglas and what she had done there and how she had gone on to Glen Trool. The sergeant made notes in a notebook while the constable stood by and watched him, and Lucas stood by the window of the sitting room of the cottage looking out at the view. The sergeant then asked her if anyone had known she would be out all afternoon.

'Well, no,' she answered, 'I didn't tell anyone before I left.'

'What about your drive up to Glen Trool? Did you tell Mr Austin you would be going there?'

'Yes, I think I did.'

It was when the sergeant asked her if she had any suspicions about who might have vandalised the cottage that she told him about the figures she had seen creeping about in the garden the night before and how she had challenged them and had followed them. Soon after making notes about that he said he would make some tests for fingerprints on some of the broken furniture and on the doors. When that had been done he made sure he could get in touch with her again through Lucas, and he and the constable left.

In the sitting room Kathy looked around dispiritedly at the slashed armchairs and sofa and the torn curtains. Only a few days ago she and Polly had stood in this room, pleased with how it had looked after all the efforts to renovate it. Now it was destroyed.

How could she possibly live in this house knowing it had been ravished by strangers? Andrew's cottage that he had willed to her had been vandalised and his photograph had been irreparably damaged, so that it seemed to her the few slender links she had had with him had been cut in spite of her efforts to preserve them.

'What am I going to do now?' It came out in a sigh of despondency. 'Where am I going to stay? Where am I going to live?'

Lucas turned from the window and looked across at her.

'You can stay with me,' he said brusquely.

'But. . .'

'No buts,' he said firmly. 'You'll stay tonight at my house. The least I can do is offer you somewhere to stay until you've got over the shock of this and can think straight again and decide what it is you want to do. Come on, I'll help you pack up some clothes.'

They went up to Kathy's bedroom and he opened the wardrobe door, which had been splintered with an axe. When they both saw what had been done to her clothes they stared in speechless horror for a few moments. Legs of pants had been chopped off and sleeves had been wrenched out of jackets and dresses.

'Oh, no! No!' gasped Kathy. 'Oh, what am I going to do?' She sank down on the edge of the damaged bed. Seeing her clothes hacked to pieces so vengefully was the last straw.

'You can't give in now,' said Lucas harshly. 'Really, Kathy, I thought you had more spunk than this! Collect up the clothes that aren't damaged and pack them in this.' He dragged out one of her suitcases which fortunately had not been damaged. 'And while you're doing that I'll go and find something to bar the front door with,' he added.

He left the room and, moving sluggishly, Kathy did what he had told her to do, packing underwear and blouses that she took from the chest of drawers which for some reason hadn't been touched. When she had finished she carried the case downstairs. Lucas was hammering nails into two bars of wood which he had placed across the front doorway so that the door couldn't be opened inwards.

They went out by the back door, making sure it was locked. Lucas carried her case and in silence they walked along the path through the bushes and the rowan trees. It was a beautiful evening. The air was soft and scented. The windows of Rowans brimmed with reflected golden light from the setting sun and on a nearby tree a thrush whistled its repetitive evening song.

But Kathy had never felt so desolate in her life. All her planning, all her efforts to make a life for herself, to go it on her own, had come to nothing after all. She seemed to be right back at square one, and the future looked empty and bleak.

CHAPTER SIX

IT wasn't until they were in the house and she was following Lucas across the hallway and into the living room that Kathy roused herself sufficiently to speak her mind when she realised suddenly that she was about to do what she had decided not to do.

'I can't stay here with you for another night,' she announced abruptly. 'I'll go to the hotel.'

Lucas turned to face her, his back to the windows through which sunlight was streaming.

'You won't get a room there, not tonight. Every room is booked. There's a race meeting on of the National Association of Argos dinghies, and the yacht club here is playing host to participants from all over Scotland so the hotel is full,' he replied.

'Then I'll go into Kilburn and stay at the hotel there. I can't stay here with you.'

'Why not?'

'Oh, you know why I can't,' she said wearily.

'For the same reason you decided not to come sailing with me, I suppose,' he suggested dryly.

'Yes. I can't do it, Lucas. I can't have an affair with you. I can't sleep with you. I'm not that sort of woman—I can't do it without some sort of commitment.'

'Commitment?' he queried, raising his eyebrows. 'Oh, you mean marriage, I suppose,' he

went on with a touch of mockery. 'All right—
forget that I ever made the suggestion that we
should have an affair, as you call it. Put it right out
of your mind. Now does that make it easier for
you to accept my hospitality for a night or two
while you decide what it is you want to do about
Seaview? Can you now accept my invitation in
the spirit it's offered, as one neighbour to
another? You can't stay at The Moorings and I
wouldn't recommend the hotel in Kilburn to
anyone. I have a spare bedroom and you're
welcome to it.'

'But you said that last night, and . . . and
looked what happened then,' she pointed out.
'No, I can't stay with you. I appreciate your
invitation, but I don't want everyone in the
village thinking I've become a member of your
harem. . .'

'My what?' Lucas's eyes flashed angrily and he
stepped towards her menacingly. 'What did you
say?' he demanded, towering over her.

'Your . . . your harem,' she repeated, refusing
to back down. 'I don't want to be regarded as one
of the women who live around here that you've
had an affair with.'

'What the hell are you talking about? What
gossip have you been listening to?' he demanded
harshly. 'Who's been telling lies about me to
you?' He broke off, his eyes narrowing dangerously, then added, 'Oh, I think I can guess. You
had lunch with him, didn't you? Mike Austin.
Well, I'd like to know exactly what he said about
me and to have the chance to deny or affirm it.
No person in this country is guilty until it's been

proven, and you know that. So you're going to tell me right now what your late husband's cousin has been saying about me and give me the chance to defend my good name against his slander. Sit down there.' He pointed to the sofa.

'No. I'm going to Kilburn. I ... I'll make an appointment to see you at your office on Monday,' Kathy was saying, when he advanced on her and taking hold of her by the elbows lifted her and dumped her on the sofa. He sat down beside her quickly, trapping her skirt under his thigh so that she couldn't move away and, stretching out an arm until his hand rested on the arm of the sofa, he leaned over her, barring her escape. 'You're not going anywhere until we've had this out, Kathy,' he said softly and menacingly, his eyes glittering darkly.

'You can't detain me against my will,' she spluttered as she tried to move away from him.

'But I am detaining you.'

'I could sue you for this!'

'Without witnesses? Your word against mine? No, I don't think so,' he jeered.

'Oh, you're so clever, aren't you,' Kathy muttered furiously. 'You know all the answers, all the ways of cheating the law. And you're rough, too. I would never have believed you could treat a woman so roughly!'

'I'm only rough when I'm angry,' he said, the tone of his voice deepening seductively. 'And I'm only angry with you when you behave with blind stubbornness, when you refuse to see the wood for the trees.' Raising a hand, he tucked a strand of her hair behind her ear in a gesture of affection that made her heart shake. 'But I'm not angry with you any more,' he whispered.

The subtle masculine scents of his hair and skin tantalised her nose. She could hear the steady beat of his heart and feel the hard pressure of his thigh against hers. She turned her head and found his face very near to hers, lean and shadowy, and she tingled suddenly with the desire to be kissed by him, yet still she struggled against that irresistible urge.

'Oh, Lucas, what are we going to do?' she groaned. 'We mustn't ... you mustn't ... it's wrong ... we mustn't...'

His lips touched hers in a warmly possessive kiss and her resistance collapsed immediately. She gave in at last to the great longing to have him hold her and comfort her. Lost in the pulsing warmth of his embrace, her body shaped itself to the hard thrust of his, meeting demand with demand, taking as much as giving. The room was silent save for the sound of their excited breathing, occasional groans and whispered endearments. Kathy forgot all her problems, the vandalising of the cottage, the destruction of Andrew's photograph, as the love she had once felt for Lucas, innocent and undemanding as it had been, merged with a new mature feeling that responded eagerly to the hunger for love which she sensed was raging in him.

Then far away as if in a dream she heard a bell ringing insistently.

'Telephone,' she murmured against Lucas's cheek.

'No. Front door,' he whispered. 'Let's hope whoever it is goes away.'

He turned her face to his again, their lips met and the flames of passion were igniting once more, curling along her veins, when the bell began to ring again. Still embracing, they lay quietly against each other, hearts pounding in unison as they listened and waited. The bell stopped ringing and they were just relaxing and beginning to kiss again when a voice called out.

'Hello there—Lucas! Kathy!'

'Kenny,' muttered Lucas. 'He's in the hall.' He pushed away from her, stood up, raked back his dishevelled hair and slanted a glance at her. 'You stay there,' he ordered. 'I'll see what he wants.'

He strode away towards the doorway, while Kathy swung her feet off the sofa and buttoned her blouse. She was smoothing her hair and hoping that her face wasn't too flushed when Lucas came back into the room, followed by Kenny and Lady Jane.

'Kenny said you seemed to be upset about something,' said Jane, going straight to the point as she approached the sofa. She was wearing close-fitting jeans, a striped navy blue and white cotton jersey over which she wore a casual scarlet sailcloth jacket. Her dark hair was kept in place by a hand-embroidered band worn low on the forehead. As always she was dressed in the right clothes for whatever she was or had been doing, as if she made a close study of all the right fashion magazines. Her brilliant tawny eyes blazed down critically at Kathy. 'So we thought we'd call in on our way home to see if we could help, in any way,' she went on, sitting down on the sofa. 'We saw your car parked here.'

And you just had to find out what Lucas was up to, I bet, thought Kathy acidly, but in the next instant felt glad that there had been an interruption.

'Seaview was broken into and vandalised this afternoon while I was out,' she explained as smoothly as she could. 'I came to tell Lucas and was just consulting him as to what I should do next.'

'I'll pour us some drinks while you tell them all about it,' said Lucas. 'Scotch for everyone?'

'Sounds great,' agreed Kenny, sitting down opposite to the sofa. Leaning forward, he gazed curiously at Kathy.

'With ginger ale for me, Luke darling,' Jane sang out.

'So what was destroyed at Seaview?' asked Kenny, still staring at Kathy as if she were a specimen under a microscope.

'Nearly everything,' she replied, and went on to describe the damage that had been done.

'But this is terrible!' exclaimed Jane.

'Have you called the police?' asked Kenny.

'Yes. Harrison came down right away,' said Lucas, busy pouring Scotch at the sideboard.

'Have you any idea who might have done it?' asked Jane, turning to Kathy.

'No, not really. Unless it was the men I saw last night in the garden,' Kathy said.

'What men?' exclaimed Kenny.

'I was in the kitchen making myself a bedtime drink when I heard a noise in the garden. I went outside and saw two figures. When I challenged them they ran away.'

'Seems to fit in with Ina's stories about ghosts, doesn't it?' drawled Jane thoughtfully. 'But I gather you don't believe they were ghosts.'

'I know they weren't,' asserted Kathy, taking the drink Lucas was offering to her.

'Which way did they make off?' asked Kenny.

'Along the path at the back of the house and across the lawn to this house.'

'I hope you told the police about them too,' said Kenny. 'My God, I'd no idea that there were such goings on in Redcliffe! What do you think about it, Luke? Do you think the fellows were going to break into Seaview and steal something and when Kathy surprised them and chased them off they came back this afternoon as a sort of reprisal because she frustrated them last night?'

'Could be something like that,' murmured Lucas noncommittally, poker-faced as he looked down at his drink.

'Do you know if anything was stolen this afternoon?' asked Kenny, looking across at Kathy.

'No, I don't. Somehow I never thought of theft. When I saw everything broken up. . .' She broke off with a shudder.

'What I want to know is, if the people who broke in and vandalised the cottage this afternoon were the same ones Kathy surprised last night how would they have known Kathy would be out this afternoon?' remarked Jane shrewdly, and Lucas gave her a sharp under-browed glance.

'You've got a good point there, Jane,' he said.

'Maybe they just took a chance,' said Kenny.

'Or maybe they're living somewhere in the village.' He heaved a sigh of regret. 'I'm afraid the place isn't what it used to be. We get a lot of riff-raff coming down to the public bar in the hotel now in the evenings—I daresay you've noticed, Luke. And I have heard that the police suspect some smuggling of stolen goods from the other side of the Firth to this coast is going on. My father heard that from the Commissioner of Police—they're members of the same Lodge, you know.'

'But all this isn't helping Kathy one bit,' said Jane vigorously. She turned to Kathy again. 'I really feel badly that this has happened to you after all the work you've done to make the cottage habitable again. You can't possibly stay there tonight.'

'We were discussing that when you and Ken arrived,' said Lucas. 'I've offered Kathy my spare bedroom.'

'Nice of you, Luke, but that won't do. Kathy can't stay with you. Imagine how all the old hens who live here would clack,' said Jane, shaking her head. 'No, you must come to us, Kathy. Don't you agree, Ken, that she must come and stay with us while she decides what she wants to do about the cottage?'

'I most certainly do,' said Kenny sincerely. 'We'd like you to come and stay as long as you like.'

'Thank you, it's very kind of you, but I can easily drive into Kilburn and stay at the hotel there.' As always Kathy tried to assert her independence.

'I won't hear of it,' said Kenny.

'You couldn't possibly stay in that dump,' added Jane. 'Please come and stay with us, Kathy.'

'Well, if you're sure——' began Kathy.

'Of course we're sure,' insisted Kenny. 'Tell her, Luke, old man. Advise her as her lawyer that it would be best if she comes to stay with us.'

Lucas finished the whisky in his glass before saying anything.

'Kathy will of course do as she pleases,' he said eventually in a cool, uninterested sort of voice, but the glance he gave her across the room was anything but cool. It blazed with desire and she felt her pulses quicken in response.

'That's settled, then,' said Jane briskly. 'You'll come to us, Kathy. Kenny can drive your car and you can come with me in our car. . .'

'But. . .' began Kathy. She wasn't aware that she had agreed to go with them.

'You must be feeling very shaken,' Jane swept on, 'and not feeling at all like driving. Kenny will prescribe something for you, I'm sure.'

'I really don't know why you didn't tell me when we met at the hotel,' said Kenny. 'I could sense there was something wrong—you were all dithery and your attention wasn't on what I was saying to you.'

'I'm sorry.' Kathy watched out of the corners of her eyes as Lucas got to his feet and went over to the sideboard with his empty glass. As if in obedience to a signal Jane sprang to her feet and followed him and began to talk to him urgently in a low voice. Kathy looked back at Kenny. He hadn't changed, she thought; he was still the kindly person she remembered. 'I didn't intend to be rude to you,' she told him.

'Och, you weren't rude. Just distracted and worried,' he consoled her. 'How are you feeling now?'

'Still a little upset, of course. But the shock is wearing off now.'

'I suspect Kathy is a lot tougher than any of us think she is,' said Jane, coming back to the sofa. She seemed angry about something; her mouth was set in a straight line and her eyes were glittering. 'Let's go now, shall we? Luke isn't feeling very hospitable.'

'Of course.' Kenny got to his feet obediently. 'Do you have a case somewhere, Kathy? You'll want to bring some clothes.'

'It's in the hallway.' Kathy stood up. She was glad, she told herself, very, very glad that Jane and Kenny had turned up when they had. If they hadn't turned up she would have given in completely to Lucas's domination. She would have become his illicit lover, living with him in sin, knowing all the time that he had a wife.

'I'll carry the case out to the car for you,' Kenny was saying.

'Kathy,' Lucas spoke roughly, 'don't go if you don't want to. You can stay here.'

'Don't listen to him, Kathy,' cut in Jane imperiously. 'He might not care what people say about him, but if you're going to continue to live in Redcliffe, make your home here, you don't want to give the permanent residents any reason to cold-shoulder you, do you?'

'Jane is right,' said Kenny, nodding wisely. 'Wouldn't do to have all the old crones gossiping about you. No offences intended to you, Luke, but you know how it is—it's always the women who have their reputations ripped to pieces. Kathy will be fine with us. Where did you say you put your case?'

'In the hallway, by the front door,' she replied, and Kenny left the room. She looked at Lucas. The sun was setting now and shadows were beginning to creep into the room. It wasn't easy to read the expression on his face. 'I think it's best if I go,' she said quietly. 'For both of us.' He didn't say anything but looked at her in that way which expressed quite clearly what he thought of her. He hated her even while he wanted her. Perhaps he hated her because he wanted her.

'Come on, Kathy,' said Jane. 'Kenny needs your keys for your car.'

Kathy followed Jane into the hallway, knowing that Lucas was close behind her. His anger and irritation with her seemed to vibrate through space to her, causing her nerves to twang alarmingly. She found herself tensing as she anticipated some action on his part. She felt he might at any moment take hold of her, trap her in his arms and refuse to let her follow the Smiths from the house. Swinging round she faced him.

'You must see that . . . that . . . I can't stay with you, especially now that they've invited me to stay with them. It would be wrong for me to stay with you—I know that, you know it and they know it, and . . . and soon everyone would know it. And I couldn't bear that,' she whispered defensively.

'I don't know where you've got this idea that to stay with me would be wrong,' he retorted, the words hissing between his teeth. 'Seems to me you're very changeable, blowing hot one minute and cold the next, so perhaps it is best if you go. I can manage well enough without a woman who doesn't know her own mind two minutes together!'

His hard, almost black stare was contemptuous and the curl to his lips sardonic, and even though they were standing so close to each other he had never seemed so far away. With a little moan of distress she turned and went out through the front door and down the steps to where Jane and Kenny were waiting for her. Behind her the front door was closed firmly. Lucas wasn't going to see them off.

As Jane had suggested, Kenny drove Kathy's car and she travelled with Jane in the luxuriously appointed Rover that the Smiths owned. Driving fast and expertly, Jane talked, and sitting in a half-numbed state, feeling for all the world as if she had been dragged forcibly from her natural position in life at Lucas's side and in his home, Kathy tried to listen.

'I'm so glad you're being sensible and are coming to stay at the Hall,' said Jane. 'I can't understand why Lucas offered to let you stay with him. He isn't usually so friendly or neighbourly. I suppose he feels responsible for you, being your lawyer.'

'I suppose so,' murmured Kathy, wondering

why she should feel so wretched. She hadn't wanted to stay with Lucas, so why feel miserable about leaving him?

'But then sometimes I think I'll never understand him,' continued Jane. 'I've known him for years and yet I've never been able to plumb the depths of him. We knew each other when we both lived in Edinburgh. In fact, he was in partnership with Henry Paton, my lawyer, and we met when Harry was arranging my divorce from Colin Grant, the financier.' Jane laughed softly. 'In fact, that was when I fell for Lucas.'

'Fell in love with him?' queried Kathy.

'Right. And I really think we might have made a go of it if he hadn't been married.' Jane paused, changed gear to slow down for the turn into the road that led to Clinton Hall and then went on, casually, 'But I expect you know all about his marriage.'

'No, I know nothing about it,' said Kathy stiffly. 'Is he still married?'

'Well, he hasn't said that he isn't.'

'Then where is his wife?'

'Only Lucas and God know that, and neither of them are telling,' replied Jane dryly. 'And I can tell you it was a real slap in the face for me when he told me he was still married and so he couldn't possibly marry me, when I proposed to him soon after I moved into the Hall after my father died.'

Oh, yes, thought Kathy, Jane Mortimer Smith was just the type to do the proposing. Wilful and arrogant, she would have to be the boss in any relationship. She would do all the tune-calling, and her husband or lover would have to dance to her tunes or be cast off. And being just as arrogant, Lucas wouldn't want to be married to such a woman. Poor Kenny! But then maybe he liked being told what to do. Some men liked to be married to women who would do all the organising.

'I was so put out that I turned right around and married Kenny,' continued Jane. 'Talk about going from one extreme to the other—from the arrogant, domineering hero type to the submissive anti-hero type!' She laughed mockingly. 'What was your late husband like?'

Glad of the change of subject, Kathy talked a little bit about Andrew, about how happy she had been with him and how she believed she had been doing what he had wanted her to do when she had come to Redcliffe to take over Seaview and live there.

'But now I'm not so sure I did make the right decision,' she ended rather forlornly. 'The vandals destroyed his photograph and the typewriter he gave me, as well as putting me off living in the cottage. I feel somehow as if it's been defiled by them.'

'I understand exactly how you feel,' said Jane. 'A house I once lived in was burgled while I was away, and I couldn't live in it afterwards.'

They had reached the Hall and she stopped the car in front of the entrance. In what was left of the long northern twilight of the June evening the granite walls shimmered with a ghostly violet light. Beyond the Hall the river, a ribbon of silver, sang its whispering song and the leaves of the trees rustled in the evening breeze.

'Now I do want you to make yourself at home,' said Jane generously as they walked towards the building. 'Tomorrow being Sunday, I'll be tied up at the Yacht Club helping supervise the racing programme, and I expect Kenny will be off to the Golf Club. Maybe you'd like to go with him.'

'I don't play golf,' said Kathy. 'And I'll have to go back to the cottage, to try and clean up the mess.'

'I shouldn't be in too much of a hurry to do that,' said Jane firmly. 'Have a good night's rest first, and sleep in as long as you like in the morning. Mrs Green, my housekeeper, will bring you breakfast in bed.'

'Oh no, please don't let her go to so much trouble,' protested Kathy.

'It won't be any trouble, and I know Kenny will insist that you have the best treatment. Don't forget, he regards you as an old friend. "One of the nicest of the girls who used to come on holiday to Redcliffe. Too nice for Luke MacBride," he told me,' said Jane smoothly. 'And I think maybe he's right. It was his idea that we should call in at Rowans to make sure you were all right and I have a feeling we were just in time.'

In the brightly lit wide high hallway of the Hall she turned to give Kathy a curious glance, but Kathy was saved from having to make a reply by the entrance of Kenny with her case.

'Had any supper yet, Kathy?' he asked cheerfully.

'No, there wasn't time to have anything to eat, with the police coming and . . . and everything,' she replied vaguely.

'Then we'll all have supper together now,' he said. 'Come in, come in and have another drink while Jane goes and gives her orders to Mrs Green.'

It was past ten-thirty when Kathy was shown upstairs by Jane to an elegantly furnished guest suite on the third floor of the Hall.

'I think you'll find everything you need,' Jane said. 'This suite has a bathroom and a private sitting room, so you can keep to yourself if you want to. Just treat the place as if it were your own home. Use the telephone. I expect you have relatives you'd like to call to tell them what's happened. And if there's anything else you need just ring this bell and Mrs Green will come.'

'Thank you very much. You're very kind.' Much as she appreciated Jane's generosity, Kathy was beginning to feel exhausted and was finding the other woman's attention overwhelming. The desire to be alone with her thoughts was growing desperate.

'You're most welcome. Kenny and I are really glad we've been able to help.'

And also to rescue you from the evil designs of Lucas MacBride, Kathy couldn't help thinking as the door closed behind Jane at last.

Unlocking her suitcase, she searched for and found a nightdress and began to prepare for bed, moving automatically and slowly from bedroom to bathroom and back again. She opened the small latticed window, then climbed into the comfortable double bed and switched out the light.

How different was her second coming to Clinton

Hall from her first! Was it only yesterday afternoon that she had driven here so confidently? In a little over twenty-four hours disaster had struck at her. Her home had been vandalised, and now she felt as if someone had deliberately knocked the ladder on which she had been standing from beneath her, causing her to fall.

She flung over on to her back and looked through the window at the stars twinkling in the dark blue sky, her thoughts swinging inevitably to the previous night when she had got up and had surprised the men in the garden and then had chased them to Lucas's lawn.

Part of last night she had spent making love and sleeping with Lucas, and tonight the same would have happened if the Smiths hadn't arrived when they had.

'Kathy, don't go if you don't want to go,' Lucas had said.

So why hadn't she stayed? Because for all she loved him and wanted to be with him she still didn't trust him. And now she knew she had been right not to trust him. Now she knew for sure he was still married and that the story Mike had told her about Lucas having a wife in hospital was probably true.

But why hadn't Lucas told her the truth about himself? Why, instead of telling her had he made love to her? Because he hadn't wanted her to know the truth. He hadn't wanted to tell her he was still married.

And now she was all mixed up, her body aching to be with him while her mind declared she was glad she had escaped from him; loving him with every fibre of her being, yet fearing the power he had over her physical responses, knowing that if she gave in to his lovemaking again she would cease to be in control of her own life. She would become his possession, his mistress.

And if that were the case wouldn't it be best if she sold Seaview and left Redcliffe never to return? On that negative thought she fell asleep suddenly, emotionally exhausted.

Next morning the sky was clear, the sun was shining and a pleasant breeze was blowing. After telling Mrs Green where she was going and when she would return to the Hall, Kathy drove straight to Seaview Cottage. Outside her car she stood for a few moments looking at the estuary. It was almost noon and the tide was slowly making, sliding in over the mudbanks. Near the jetty people were moving about attending to the many dinghies that were parked near it, preparing no doubt for the next race which would start when the tide was half in. She glanced at the deep pool where the bigger boats were moored. Lucas's boat wasn't there. He must have left possibly at first light on the ebbing tide, and she felt a sudden raw ache of regret because she couldn't be with him.

'Forget it, forget him,' she chided herself, and going round to the back of the house she unlocked the door and stepped inside the kitchen. If she had really wanted to go sailing with Lucas she would have gone with him yesterday, wouldn't she? She had to stop behaving like a pendulum swinging this way and that. Or stop blowing hot and cold, as Lucas had called her behaviour. She had to make up her mind what it was she wanted to do and stick to her decision.

And she had made up her mind. Before she had left Clinton Hall she had phoned her parents and had told them what had happened. They had advised her to leave Redcliffe and go to them, and she had agreed to do that on Monday after she had cleared up the mess at the cottage today. It would be easier for her to decide what to do with the cottage if she was away from it, in particular if she was away from the powerful influence of Lucas.

In the kitchen she surveyed the broken furniture with sinking spirits, tempted to leave there and then, to lock the back door, get into her car and drive straight to Manchester. But that wasn't her way. She had to make some attempt to tidy up and to salvage some of her belongings. She would start with the bedroom.

She had done all she could with the bedroom and had packed the rest of her torn and hacked clothes in her other cases and was trying to restore order to the kitchen when she heard a knock on the front door, and looking out of the front window she saw a blue delivery van with the name Austin Ltd printed on it parked behind her car. Mike had come, and she belatedly remembered the record player. In the hallway she shouted through the barred door:

'Go round to the back door!'

He heard her and shouted back:

'Okay!'

When he stepped into the kitchen he whistled in surprise at the broken furniture.

'What happened?' he exclaimed. 'Looks like a tornado has been through here!' He slanted her a mocking light brown glance. 'Or did you throw a wild party last night? You might have invited me.'

'It wasn't a tornado and it wasn't a wild party. It happened yesterday afternoon while I was out. Someone broke in and smashed up everything,' Kathy told him.

'They certainly did a good job,' he remarked, looking around. 'Who? Any idea who did it?'

'No. Unless. . .' She broke off, wondering whether to tell him about Kenny's theory that the vandals might also have been the two figures she had seen in the garden the previous night.

'Go on,' he urged cautiously.

'Oh, it was just a suggestion that was made by someone that the men I saw Friday night creeping about the garden and whom I chased might have come back and wrecked everything because they couldn't find anything to steal.'

'You didn't tell me about seeing two men in the garden,' he complained. 'Why didn't you?'

'I suppose I forgot,' she admitted. 'It was just like your friend Keith described to you. They ran away along the path and across the lawn at Rowans and. . .'

'And disappeared into MacBride's house?' he suggested eagerly.

'No, they didn't go into his house—at least, he said they didn't. I went and knocked on his door to ask him.'

'Easy enough for him to deny that they were there.'

'I know. But they weren't there,' Kathy said firmly. Mike leaned against the partly demolished dresser and stared at her with narrowed eyes.

'I suppose you've told the police about this,' he said.

'Yes. They were here yesterday evening examining everything, testing for fingerprints.'

'I see.' He frowned and chewed at his lower lip. 'What are you going to do now?'

'Finish tidying up, lock the door and go back to Manchester. I'm sorry, Mike, I won't be needing the record player after all.'

'You mean you're not going to live here?' There was a strange lilt in his voice. She had the impression he sounded hopeful.

'I don't think so. This vandalism has turned me off the place. They destroyed some things I valued very much.' Her voice shook a little. 'It seems as if they destroyed a part of my life, a part I treasure very much, so I think it would be best if I left.'

'Och, now, that's a pity, so it is—a great pity,' he mourned. 'Just when you and I were getting to know each other. Will you sell the cottage?'

'I don't know yet. I have to think about it and get some advice.'

'Well, I'll give you some good advice now. Whatever you do don't sell to MacBride,' Mike said urgently. 'Sell it to me. I've more right to it than he has—more than you have, really. I'm just as much John Reid's nephew as Andrew was, so bear me in mind when you're thinking of getting rid of it.'

'I will—I promise,' she replied.

'Now is there anything I can do for you while I'm here?'

'You can help me to clear up. I'm so glad you've come—I was beginning to wonder how I was going to pick up every piece of shattered glass and every piece of broken crockery.'

It was almost five o'clock when they finished and Mike said he had to leave to meet a friend in Dumfries. He asked Kathy where she would be staying the night.

'I'm staying with the Smiths at Clinton Hall. I'll be driving south tomorrow.'

'Then I suppose this is goodbye.' Mike managed to look regretful.

'For the time being.'

'I'm really sorry you're going.' He looked down at her with eyes that were very like Andrew's yet were not quite. They were set much closer together than Andrew's had been, giving Mike's face a ferrety look, and they didn't smile to hide a certain sadness.

'Are you?' Kathy retorted lightly. 'But there's no reason why we shouldn't meet again. I mean, if I do decide to sell the cottage to you I'll have to come up to sign papers and we could meet then.'

'That's right, we could,' he agreed, but he didn't sound too enthusiastic. 'Well, I must be off. Been nice knowing you, Kathy. Cheerio!'

When he had gone she collected the suitcases she had packed and carried them out to her car. Dinghies were still racing on the estuary, sails fluttering when they went about, coloured spinnakers ballooning out when they rounded a mark and ran before the breeze. In the Deep Pool Lucas's boat was still absent from its mooring.

She drove away from Seaview without a backward look and went straight to the hotel to find Polly and Harry to tell them what had happened. They were appalled.

'But you'll never let it drive you away from Redcliffe,' said Polly. 'You'll come back and do the place up again and live in it, I'm sure you will. It'll take time for you to get over the shock, but you'll be back.'

'No, I don't think so somehow,' said Kathy sadly. Knowing Lucas was married to a woman who needed him more than she did, she would never come back.

Later that evening at the Hall she joined the informal supper party that Kenny and Jane had organised for Yacht Club members and guests to celebrate the end of the racing. It was a good way to pass the evening and prevented Kathy from brooding too much on her present situation. She found that she knew some of the guests; they had been members of the Yacht Club when she had sailed with Lucas nine years previously. They all commiserated with her over the vandalism at Seaview, which Jane had told them about, and each one had a different theory as to who might have done it.

'I wish you wouldn't leave tomorrow,' Kenny said when all the guests had left. 'Does Lucas know you're going?'

'No. He's gone sailing and hadn't returned when I left Seaview. I'll call in and see him tomorrow. I'll have to ask him to keep an eye on the place and leave the key with him,' she replied.

It was nearly one o'clock the next afternoon

when she arrived at Lucas's office, having failed to find him at Rowans. As she climbed the stairs she grinned wryly to herself. Since she had last climbed them her life had been turned upside down. Or was it inside out? At any rate everything was different.

Yet when she opened the door to the outer office she felt that nothing had changed, because the room was just the same. The African violets still flowered profusely and Mrs Murray was wearing the same red suit and the corrugated waves of her hair still glinted brassily.

'Mrs Reid?' queried Mrs Murray brightly.

'That's right.'

'Do you have an appointment with Mr MacBride?'

'No, I don't, but I wondered if. . .'

'He isn't here, and he's not expected in until later this afternoon. Come back around three.'

'Oh, I couldn't do that,' said Kathy. 'You see, I'm on my way to Manchester. I'm expected there this evening and I'd like to be on the road to Carlisle as soon as possible. Perhaps I could leave a note for Mr MacBride and the key to Seaview Cottage?'

'Just as you like. Would you like to dictate your message for him and I'll type it out for you.'

'That's a good idea. Just put this: "I've decided to go and stay with my parents for a while. As soon as I've decided what to do with the cottage I'll write to you. Please keep an eye on the place. I've left the key."'

Mrs Murray's fingers danced over the keys of the typewriter and Kathy watched admiringly,

wishing she could type as fast and as accurately.
When the note was typed she signed it. She put
the keys of Seaview down on Mrs Murray's desk,
said goodbye and left, half hoping she would
meet Lucas on the stairs, in the Town Hall
entrance or even on the street outside.

But she didn't see him anywhere, and feeling
suddenly lonely and unwanted, she hurried to her
car and drove away from Kilburn quickly before
she could change her mind and climbed back up
the stairs to the offices of Kelvin, Morris and
MacBride to tell Mrs Murray she would wait for
Mr MacBride after all.

Better to leave without seeing him again. Better
never to see him again. Better for both of them.

CHAPTER SEVEN

MISTY grey rain shrouded the sky, the low green hills, the dark pine woods, the scattered farmhouses, and the uniform greyness of everything seemed to Kathy to be expressive of her feelings. Inside she was misty and grey too. Yet only a few weeks ago when she had travelled this road in the opposite direction on the bus she had been so full of hope, her spirits soaring blue and gold as the blustery May day had been then. Then she had been determined to start a new life for herself; a life in which she had hoped to be totally independent both financially and emotionally. Falling in love again with Lucas MacBride was the last thing she had expected to happen to her. And now she was running away from that love, afraid that it might involve her in an immoral situation with him.

Houses began to appear on either side of the road, the damp red sandstone houses of Maxwelltown. Down to the bridge over the River Nith and up the other side into the city of Dumfries. By three o'clock, the time Lucas was expected back at his office by Mrs Murray, Kathy was thirty miles away from Kilburn and entering the town of Annan.

Half an hour later she was nearer to Gretna Green than to Annan when she heard an ominous clunking sound coming from the back of the car.

The vehicle began to lurch about, and guessing she had a flat tyre she guided the car on to the shoulder of road and stopped the engine. Beside her a five-barred gate guarded the entrance to a wide potato field edged on one side by a plantation of trees. There was no sign of habitation, just fields and woods stretching away into the wet mist.

Pulling on her raincoat, she fastened it, got out of the car and walked to the rear of it. The rear tyre on the right side was as flat as a pancake. Sighing, she opened the boot of the car and managed, after a struggle, to drag out the spare wheel. Then she found the jack and wheelbrace. By the time she had lifted everything out her hair was wet and straggling around her ears and her legs had been splashed with spray from the wheels of passing cars that didn't slow down on that straight stretch of road.

She tugged off the hub-cap, attached the wheelbrace to a nut and began to turn the brace, thankful that she had once taken an evening course in car maintenance way back in Edmonton. But nothing happened as she turned. No matter how hard she pushed and pulled on the brace the nut didn't shift. She tried the next nut, with the same result, and so on all the way round the hub of the wheel. All the nuts seemed to have rusted into place and they refused to budge.

Breathing deeply as she controlled a childish desire to kick the offending wheel, Kathy pushed back her hair and looked back the way she had come. Nothing there. Only the flat grey tarmac stretching into mist. No car coming and no driver she could flag down and ask for help. She would just have to try with the wheelbrace again.

She was bent over the brace and grunting as she leaned all her weight on it when a car going fast, exceeding the speed limit, went by, its wheels throwing up spray that drenched her back and legs. Immediately she straightened up and shouted a few rude words after the car, biting back more curses when she realised it was stopping with a screech of brakes and tyres on the wet road. While she stared the car began to reverse on to the shoulder, backing up and stopping a few yards in front of her car. It was long, low and grey. It was a Jaguar.

A door opened, a man got out, slammed the door and began to stride towards her. He was wearing a short waterproof jacket open over a grey suit and his black hair was soon shiny with rain. He walked right up to her as she stood with the wheelbrace dangling from her hand, her mouth slightly open with surprise.

'Lucas! What are you doing here?' she exclaimed, and felt the old familiar leap of her heart.

'I'm chasing you,' he replied, his mouth twisting wryly. 'God knows why.' His glance slanted to the flat tyre. 'Seems you have a problem.'

'I can't shift any of the nuts,' she explained. 'They all seem to be rusted in place.' She gave him a diffident glance. His face was set in grim lines and he looked most unapproachable. 'I . . . don't suppose you would try to shift them for me?' she queried, fully prepared to be rebuffed.

She was. He gave her a cold appraising glance, taking in her wet hair, her wet face and her drenched raincoat.

'You suppose right,' he retorted. 'I won't try to shift them for you in this weather.'

'Oh—why not?' she demanded, suddenly losing her diffidence and becoming irritated with him.

'Because if I do and you're able to put on the spare wheel you'll then get in your car and drive on and I'll have to follow you again until you decide to stop somewhere.'

'I don't understand,' she complained. 'Why have you followed me?'

'To ask you to return to Kilburn.' He wiped drops of rain from his face with the back of one hand. 'We're both getting soaked standing here. Come to my car and sit down and I'll explain to you.'

Kathy thought she had left him far behind. She had vowed to herself never to see him again. But here he was standing before her, exerting that power he had over her. She could feel his arrogance emanating from him, encircling her, threatening to engulf her, and yet still she had to resist it.

'I'd prefer to change this wheel first,' she replied stubbornly, and bending down, she fitted the wheelbrace to a nut.

With a deftly aimed kick of one foot Lucas sent the brace flying from her hands, to land with a clatter a few yards away. Losing her balance, she sat down suddenly on the wet ground. She glared up at him, but he wasn't there. He was pushing up the lid of the boot which she hadn't locked, having left her keys dangling from the lock. He picked up the spare wheel and threw it in the boot, and while she struggled to get to her feet she heard the jack and the wheelbrace clang as he threw them into the boot too. Then the lid was slammed shut.

'Why did you do that?' She stepped towards him, intending to snatch her keys from his hand, but he sidestepped neatly, opened the nearest rear door of the car, reached into the back seat, hauled out two of her suitcases, slammed the door shut and then still with her keys in his hand and carrying the two cases he marched off towards his own car.

'Lucas, come back here at once!' she shouted after him, but he didn't even turn to look back at her. 'Oh, really! Some men!' she muttered darkly and fiercely, and began to march after him. She had just reached his car when he started back towards hers, having put her cases in the boot of his car and shut it. 'Now what are you going to do?' she demanded, skidding to a stop as he strode past her.

'Get your other case and lock up your car,' he replied briskly, and strode on.

'But I can't leave it here,' she argued, following him with never a thought as to how wet she was getting or how ridiculous their behaviour might seem to an onlooker—if there had been any onlookers on that deserted stretch of road.

By the time she caught up with him he had her third case out of the back seat and was locking doors.

'Lucas! This is . . . is . . . well, it's silly. You can't kidnap me like this,' she flared. 'Give me my keys!'

He didn't answer her but having locked all the doors of her car he started to stride back to his own car. Wet and furious, feeling that he was treating her as if she was one of those helpless women who can't do anything for themselves, Kathy dithered for a moment between her car and his, only turning to run towards his when she heard its engine start up.

Opening the door on the left side, she flung herself down on the comfortable bucket seat and slammed the door as hard as she could, making sure that he knew how angry she was with him.

'Fasten the seat-belt,' he ordered coldly, and releasing the handbrake he swung the steering wheel. The car did a one-eighty-degree turn and then shot forward in the direction of Annan. Hastily Kathy buckled the belt about her.

'I don't want to go back to Kilburn,' she said rather breathlessly. 'I don't see why I should. You said you'd explain why. You didn't say you'd . . . you'd trick me into getting into your car and then kidnap me. Stop the car now—immediately! Stop it and tell me why you're taking me back to Kilburn.'

'I'll tell you, but I'm not stopping,' he said curtly. 'The police would like to interview you again about the break-in. Sergeant Harrison wants you to identify someone. He called me into the police station to see him just after lunch. He asked me where you were staying and if it would be possible for you to go into the station this afternoon. I phoned Clinton Hall and Jane told me you'd already left for Manchester. I went to the office to look up your address in Manchester, and Agnes gave me your message. She said I'd missed you by about twenty minutes, so I decided to chase you and hope to catch up with you.' He slanted her a glance. 'It took some doing! Do you always drive as if the police are after you?'

'I keep within the speed limit, which is more than you do,' she retorted, noting how fast the car was rushing by fields, trees and the odd house. 'Who does Sergeant Harrison want me to identify?'

'He'll explain when we get to the police station,' Lucas replied noncommittally.

Kathy slumped back in her seat, kicking off her wet shoes and wriggling her toes in an effort to warm up her cold feet. Surprisingly she felt disappointed. Lucas had followed her not on his own behalf but because Sergeant Harrison wanted to see her. She couldn't help wishing he had come after her on his own account, because he had decided he loved her and couldn't live without her even though he had a wife shut away in a mental hospital. Oh, how foolishly romantic she was, wishing he was Mr Rochester and she was Jane Eyre!

'Last night at a party Jane and Kenny gave for some of their sailing friends someone suggested that the men I saw creeping about the garden at Seaview might have been real smugglers not ghosts of smugglers, who have been using the cottage as a place to drop off stolen goods smuggled across the estuary,' she said. 'Do you think they might have been?'

'They might have been,' he replied coolly, noncommittal again.

She glanced at him. His profile, steep slope of forehead, bold rather beaky nose, hard jutting chin, was stone-like, giving nothing away.

'I think you know they were,' she stated. 'I think you've known all the time that the place was being used as a drop-off.'

'Are you going to start accusing me again of harbouring smugglers?' he jeered.

'No, I'm not. But I am accusing you of knowing that the cottage has been used by smugglers. You knew before I moved into the cottage, but you never said anything to me.'

'I did try to put you off going to live in it,' he said smoothly, and took the time to flick her another dark glance. 'But you wouldn't be put off. As I've told you before, you're very stubborn when you set your mind on doing something. Only a lot of shouting or application of force will make you change direction. Andrew Reid must have had a hell of a time living with you.'

'Oh, there you go, getting personal again, distracting me because you don't want to tell me the truth about the smugglers ... or anything else!' she accused angrily. 'Well, for your information, Andrew was a kind, loving, generous person and he never once asked me to change direction. In fact he encouraged me always to do what I wanted to do. Always. And he never shouted at me, lied to me, picked me up and threw me on a sofa. Nor did he ever kick me!'

'I didn't kick *you*. I kicked the wheelbrace out of your hands. And if I hadn't you'd still be there back on the road snivelling because you couldn't undo the nuts.'

'I wasn't snivelling,' she argued, and heaved around in the seat so that she couldn't see him any more, hunching her shoulder so that Lucas would be in no doubt that she didn't want to have anything to do with him for the rest of the drive.

'So Andrew took the line of least resistance, did he?' he continued mockingly. 'I suppose that's one way of dealing with a shrewish stubborn woman. But it isn't mine.'

'Obviously,' she sneered.

There was a long silence between them. The windscreen wipers swished steadily and hypnotically, the engine purred softly and music from the radio played quietly. Warmth from the heater penetrated Kathy's nylon panty hose and damp raincoat at last. Sitting up, she undid the raincoat, and noticed that they were passing through the square at Annan where lights were already twinkling from the windows of white-walled buildings.

'If you knew that the cottage was being used by smugglers why didn't you tell the police?' she asked, her lively mind returning to the argument.

'I did tell them, some time ago. But I had no hard evidence,' said Lucas. 'Since then the police and I have been watching the place. Harrison hoped he could catch the smugglers redhanded when they were making a drop. But they're a tricky lot. There's been nothing regular about their activities, no way of timing them. Harrison didn't want you to take up residence in the cottage because he thought the smugglers might not come again if they knew someone was living in it. So he asked me to try and prevent you from moving in. But his guess was wrong. They did come again, and you surprised them.'

'Just as Keith, Mike's friend, surprised them when he was living in the cottage,' she mused. 'But that was years ago.'

'Keith who?' he queried sharply.

'I don't know his last name. He's the drummer in the rock group that was playing at the village dance I went to with Mike. He told Mike about the figures he'd seen and that he'd followed, and Mike thought he'd been hallucinating.'

Lucas didn't say anything. The car purred on through the driving mist and rain. Kathy rested her head against the back of the seat. Her eyes closed and she was just slipping into a doze when Lucas said quietly,

'Mike Austin seems to have made a big hit with you.'

'Not really,' she murmured sleepily. 'I liked him at first because he reminded me of Andrew a little.'

'Enough to make you believe every word he said. Enough to believe the story he told you about his friend seeing figures disappearing into my house,' he accused harshly. 'Enough to dupe you into believing he's another nephew of John Reid. He isn't related to the Reids at all, but he managed to con old John into believing that he was.' Disgust roughened his voice even more. 'It was when I found out that there were no grandchildren descended from John Reid's uncle Angus Reid that I had Mike Austin and his gang evicted from Seaview.'

'Are you telling me that you knew Mike isn't Andrew's cousin and you never told me?' exclaimed Kathy, rousing herself to glare at him.

'Would you have believed me if I had? I seem to remember you weren't inclined to listen to me when I warned you about becoming too friendly with him.'

She was silent, remembering how easily she had been taken in by Mike's friendly overtures.

'Who is he, then?' she asked eventually.

'His name is really Mike Austin. The business in Castle Douglas in his, although he borrowed money from John Reid to get started in it, and one of the lads who vandalised your cottage works for him.'

'Oh. How do you know?'

'He dropped some visiting cards by accident. Harrison found them among the wreckage in the kitchen.'

'Visiting cards?' she queried.

'Business cards, actually. They had the name Austin Ltd printed on them and the name of the salesman in the corner. He must have had them in his shirt pocket and they fell out when he was breaking up your furniture and generally enjoying himself in his own violent fashion. Anyway, Harrison is holding him for questioning on suspicion of breaking and entering Seaview and causing damage, and he wants you to have a look at him. He thinks the salesman might have been in Austin's shop when you told Mike Austin you were going up to Glen Trool.'

'But I wasn't in the shop when I told Mike that,' she said, and then realised what that implied and caught her breath. 'Oh no!' she whispered. 'It couldn't be! Mike couldn't have had anything to do with it, could he?'

'Your guess is as good as mine,' Lucas remarked dryly. 'You told Harrison yesterday in my hearing that Mike was the only person who knew you would be out for the afternoon.'

There was another silence. In the distance the lights of Dumfries twinkled through the murk.

'I feel so foolish,' Kathy admitted at last.

'Why?'

'For believing in everything Mike said. I suppose he has connections with the smugglers.'

'Looks that way. The stuff that's being smuggled across is mostly electronics stuff, tape recorders, video casettes and the like. Easily removed from a house and easily sold again . . . as new, of course.'

'But why the vandalism?'

'To drive you away from the house, I'd suspect.'

'And he succeeded,' Kathy said dismally.

The streets of Dumfries glistened. The monument of Robbie Burns loomed up in front of the old church. The road dipped down to the bridge, crossing the misty river, then slanted up the other side and through Maxwelltown.

'I even believed what Mike said about you,' Kathy confessed.

'Did you? And what did he say about me,' asked Lucas, his voice silky soft with menace.

'You were going to tell me the other night; the night I detained you against your will, but somehow you never did.'

'Because you distracted me,' she retorted.

'And then Jane arrived and started bossing everyone about. She was furious to find you with me. But you didn't have to do what she said and go with her and Kenny. You could have stayed with me.'

'I didn't want to stay with you,' she said stiffly.

'You're not a very good liar, Katherine Warren. You never were,' he scoffed.

'I didn't want to stay with you because Mike had told me you're still married, and when Jane verified what he had said I was glad I hadn't stayed another night with you,' she said sharply. 'I've no wish to be the mistress of a man whose wife is mentally ill in hospital. I've no wish to be associated with someone as cruel as you are!'

Her words seem to fall into a deep hole of silence and were swallowed up. Lucas said nothing but drove even faster. Kathy glanced sideways at him. He was controlling his anger pretty well. Only in his lean tanned hands as they rested on the steering wheel and at his jawline did it show. Bone gleamed white through skin as muscles tensed. After a while he said in a low, savage voice,

'I hope Harrison manages to pin something on Austin. I hope he's able to jail him for several years for receiving stolen goods. It would give me great pleasure to see that bastard sent to jail!'

And after that nothing more was said by either of them until they reached Kilburn.

Kathy had always assumed that the police station lay behind the Town Hall on River Street. At least, that was where she had seen policemen going off beat and the local patrol car parked. But Lucas drove right past the Town Hall and the end of River Street, out along the main street.

'Why haven't you stopped?' she demanded. 'I thought you had to take me to the police station to identify that salesman.'

'There's no hurry for that. Tomorrow will do for that,' he replied.

'Then where are we going?'

'To a place I know of where we can dine by candlelight, talk a little and then hold hands,' he drawled. 'A place called Rowans.'

'I'm not going! Please turn around and take me back to the police station.'

'But I don't think Harrison will be there at this time of the evening. He'll be at home with his wife and kids, watching the TV or reading the local newspaper. He said tomorrow would do,' said Lucas in his smooth imperturbable lawyer's voice.

'Then take me back to my car,' she insisted.

'Now isn't that asking a little too much?' he drawled mockingly. 'I'd like to get home too and relax. Your car will be all right where it is.'

'But I'm expected at my parents' home this evening. I'll have to get in touch with them, tell them I've been delayed. Detained,' she added as an afterthought, giving him an accusing glare, 'against my will.'

'You can phone them from Rowans.'

'But I don't want to go to Rowans. Lucas, will

you stop riding roughshod over my wishes! Will you stop trying to take over and run my life for me. I've told you. . .'

'I know,' he interrupted her roughly. 'You don't want to be associated with me because I'm cruel and because Mike Austin told you I have a wife in a mental hospital. But you have to admit that you're damp and hungry, so we'll go to Rowans and you can have a hot bath and change while I cook dinner for us. And then . . .' he paused tantalisingly.

'Then what?'

'Then maybe you will allow me to put you straight on one or two items about my private life and personal relationships, since you're so interested,' he drawled icily.

'Oh, all right,' she muttered ungraciously. 'But you really are very domineering.'

'It strikes me you need someone to domineer you,' he retorted. 'You need someone who'll watch out for you and prevent you from being deceived by smooth operators like Mike Austin.'

'But he does look a little like Andrew,' she flared up defensively.

For answer he gave her a sidelong glance of pure scorn and the car sped along the wet road, past drenched fields and under dripping trees. Barrochburn was a single street of ghostly grey cottages. The corner where the road to Redcliffe joined the main road was flooded and the car wheels churned up a wide swathe of water as the car skidded round it, and Redcliffe's church steeple looked more severe than ever, dark and bleak against the misty grey sky.

Rowans was dark too, but somehow warm and welcoming when they stepped inside. The front door closed behind them. Lucas flicked on lights to disperse the grey gloom and turned towards Kathy. Two evenings ago they had stood in the same place looking at each other and tension had twanged between them. It was twanging again almost unbearably for her.

'Kathy,' Lucas murmured, his voice deepening, his eyes growing even darker, their expression softening as he stepped towards her.

'No—no. Not yet. Not yet,' she whispered, backing away from him. 'You said you'd put me straight on a few items first. You said I could bathe and change and you'd cook dinner. You mustn't rush me, Lucas, please. Oh, don't come any nearer, don't kiss me. I'll never forgive you if you kiss me now!'

He was still advancing, his eyes gleaming with wicked mockery, as she backed away, and he had just placed his hands on her waist and she had just raised her hands to his chest to push him away when the front door bell rang, ironically, so it seemed to Kathy. Lucas's head jerked back, his mouth twisted in exasperation and he frowned.

'What the hell?' he muttered, and letting go of her strode past her to the door and swung it open.

'Thank God you're home at last, Luke!' Jane Mortimer Smith's voice rang out imperiously. 'I've been hanging about for nearly half an hour waiting to see your car turn into the lane.'

Kathy swung round. As she was talking Jane was stepping past Lucas and into the hallway.

'I had to come, Luke,' Jane went on, not seeing

Kathy and turning back to Lucas, who was still standing by the open door, the expression on his face enigmatic. 'You see, it's happened at last—what I've been hoping might happen. Kenny has walked out at last. He's left me. We had a really noisy row and he left.' Jane suddenly launched herself at Lucas, twining her arms around his neck. 'Oh, darling, I wanted you to be the first to know. Kenny's left me, so now there's nothing to stop us from being together. I'll divorce him and then we'll get married. . .'

'But what about Lucas's wife?' Kathy heard her own voice speaking coldly and clearly. 'How can you marry him? He's still married to another woman.'

With an exclamation of surprise Jane spun round to face Kathy. In her pale face, framed by the upturned collar of her elegant white trench-coat, her eyes blazed yellow. A scarf of scarlet silk was tied over her dark hair.

'You?' she spat between taut scarlet lips. 'I thought you'd left too, for good. I thought we'd got rid of you!' She swung back to Lucas. 'What's she doing here?' she demanded.

'Kathy is here because I went after her and brought her back,' Lucas replied coolly. He closed the front door, then added smoothly, 'If you'd like to step into the living room, Mrs Smith, I'll be with you in a few minutes.'

'Lucas, you can't treat me in this way, as if . . . as if I were one of your clients. I haven't come here to consult you professionally!' shrilled Jane. Ignoring her, he stepped past her, picked up the suitcase Kathy had chosen to bring indoors with her and crossing over to her said quietly, with a sort of grim politeness,

'I'll show you where the spare bedroom is.'

'I can go to The Moorings,' she whispered.

'You're staying here,' he said autocratically. 'If you really want to help your old friend Kenny to save his marriage you'll do as I ask and go up to the spare bedroom now, have a bath and change while I deal with her.' He jerked his head in Jane's direction, the expression on his face one of contempt.

'Oh, all right . . . if you're sure it's in Kenny's interests.'

'I'm sure.'

'Lucas, Kathy can't stay here!' Jane was in action again, coming towards them.

Lucas turned slowly to look at her.

'Shut up and go into the living room,' he ordered icily. 'I've had enough of your interference in my affairs. Now do as I say and I'll come to you after I've seen Kathy upstairs. Or get out.'

'How . . . how dare you speak to me like that!' spluttered Jane, and then much to Kathy's surprise she burst into tears and turning on her heel ran across the hallway into the living room.

'Oh, dear,' said Kathy with a sigh. 'Perhaps you'd better go to her now.'

'Do her good to wait,' Lucas said curtly. 'Come on, this way.'

They went up a short flight of stairs to the second level of the split-level house and he led her to a spacious bedroom furnished with twin beds, Scandinavian type chests of drawers and a couple of armchairs.

'You can get to the bathroom through that door,' he indicated a slightly open door. 'So make yourself comfortable and take your time.'

'I don't understand,' protested Kathy, following him to the doorway of the bedroom. 'Do you think Kenny has really left her? He seemed so fond of her. No, not just that. He seemed to be deeply in love with her.'

'He is. And in her own way she loves him.'

'She told me she's in love with you.'

'Did she? I wonder why?' Lucas shrugged his shoulders dismissingly, giving nothing away as usual. 'Have that bath and change your clothes while I get rid of Jane. I'll come up and tell you when dinner is ready.'

He went out and closed the door. Alone, Kathy stood for a moment hesitating. Now was her chance, she thought, to leave this house while Lucas was talking with Jane in the living room. Now she could creep down the few stairs across the hallway and let herself out of the front door. In a few minutes she could be at The Moorings.

At that moment she caught sight of herself in a long mirror on the clothes closest door and her eyes widened in surprise at what she saw. She looked a mess, her hair hanging down in twisted wet tails, her raincoat, not an expensive trenchcoat like Jane's but a thin easily stowed one, was creased and covered with damp patches and drooped about her. Her face was white and her eyes seemed to have sunk into their sockets. She couldn't possibly arrive at The Moorings looking like a bedraggled cat! It would be best if she first availed herself of Lucas's hospitality, took a bath, shampooed and dried her hair and changed her clothes and shoes.

Half an hour later, washed and dried, her hair smooth and shining, she dressed in a different skirt and sweater. She re-packed her suitcase, slung her raincoat about her shoulders, picked up her case and tiptoed to the bedroom door. Her hand curved about the brass doorknob. She turned it and pulled. The door stayed closed, so she pulled again harder. The door didn't budge. It had been locked from the other side.

CHAPTER EIGHT

KATHY stared incredulously at the flat cream-painted door. She couldn't believe that Lucas had deliberately locked her in the room. Several times she tugged at the doorknob thinking that perhaps the door had jammed in the opening, that perhaps it had swollen with damp and the frame was warped. But it wasn't jammed. It was locked.

Then she remembered the bathroom. There was a door opening out of that on to the landing. She hurried over to the smaller room. It was still steamy from the bath she had taken. She tried the landing door. It was also locked.

'Oh, damn!' she muttered crossly, and kicked at the panel of the door. 'Lucas MacBride, you are the most devious, the most arrogant, the most medieval man I know!'

Suddenly she saw the funny side of the situation and began to laugh. It was like an incident out of one of her novels, the wicked hero-villain capturing the tempestuous wilful heroine, carrying her off to his castle and locking her up when she showed signs of refusing to submit to his amorous advances.

But this wasn't the Middle Ages and Rowans wasn't a castle. It was the twentieth century, and Rowans was a very modern split-level bungalow and its windows were not very high up. She should be able to get out of one of them, jump to the ground and be off to The Moorings.

Going to one of the bedroom windows, she drew back the heavy folk-weave curtains. The window was wide and double-glazed, two panes of glass, one of which slid back over the other when the catch was released. Cool damp air drifted in through the mesh of the insect screen when she had opened the window. She would have to remove the screen before she could climb out.

She peered through the mesh. Although the light was poor there were still a few hours to sunset and darkness and she could see the lawn stretching away to the trees and shrubs behind Seaview. She could even see the chimneys of the cottage. The building really did block the view of the river from this house.

But somehow she must try to remove the screen. If it was like the screens she had been used to in Canada it should lift off quite easily . . . from the outside. And it did seem to be like the ones she was used to, because no amount of pushing and plucking from the inside would shift it.

She closed the window and drew the curtains then turned to look at the pleasant room. Perhaps it would be better to stay here in comfort and wait for Lucas to unlock the door and let her out. Anyway, she wanted to hear his explanations; she wanted to hear his story about his wife.

There was everything in that room to make a guest's stay comfortable; books, a cassette player and a variety of cassettes. But Kathy was too restless to read or listen. She longed to know if Jane was still in the house.

Perhaps she shouldn't have told Lucas about

Jane being in love with him. Perhaps he hadn't known until she had told him, and now that he did know his attitude to the other woman would be different. A man's behaviour towards a woman often changed when he realised that woman loved him, and wasn't it possible that Lucas was now taking advantage of Jane's love for him and, isntead of giving her advice on how to be reconciled to Kenny, was making love to her down there in the living room?

Oh, no, she wasn't having that going on while she was locked in this room. Striding over to the door, she began to hit it with one fist.

'Lucas! Lucas!' she shouted. 'The door's locked. Come and let me out. Let me out! Let me out! Lucas—Lucas!'

She pounded at the door and shouted until her fist felt sore and her voice was hoarse, then she went to sit in one of the armchairs. She was no longer amused by the situation; she was feeling furious with Lucas again.

At last she heard the lock slide back. The door opened and Lucas came in. His suit jacket was off and he had taken off his tie and opened his shirt collar. His dark eyes glimmered with mockery in the lamplight.

'Did I hear you call me?' he asked.

'You certainly did!' Kathy flung at him, and grabbing suitcase and raincoat she made for the door. 'I don't know what you're playing at, locking me in this room,' she fumed, walking right into him as he stepped in front of her.

'I suspected you might try to leave while I was talking to Jane and I didn't want to have to go chasing all over the countryside looking for you again,' he said sternly. 'Now let me take that from you.' He wrenched the suitcase from her hand. 'Dinner is just about ready.'

'And Jane? Is she staying for dinner too?' She glowered at him.

'No, she's gone. I phoned Kenny and he came and picked her up.' He smiled suddenly, the wickedly attractive corner-of-the-mouth-smile that mocked her. 'You wouldn't be jealous of her, by any chance, would you?' he suggested softly.

'No. No, of course not. Why should I be? I . . . I'm not in love with Kenny,' she retorted, giving him a disdainful glance.

'I didn't think you were,' remarked Lucas, still with a glimmer of a smile. 'So will you come to dinner now that you know she's gone?'

'I suppose so,' she muttered.

He dropped her suitcase inside the room and led the way to the stairs and down and along a passage to the dining annexe. An oval table was set with handwoven tablemats, shining silverware and cut-glass. Two candles in tall candleholders flickered with golden light.

The meal was simple enough, a seafood casserole with rice and a mixed salad, followed by fresh fruit and cheese, and there was a light white wine to go with it. Kathy ate hungrily without speaking, and the silence was broken only by the sound of orchestral music coming from the living room. But as the meal progressed the silence became rather tense, until Lucas threw down his serviette and said irritably,

'It's good to have you here, Kathy, but it

would be better if you would relax and stop being so damned stiff and starchy.'

'I'm not being stiff and starchy,' she replied. 'I just can't think of anything to say to you ... except to ask questions which you'll probably resent and will refuse to answer.'

'How do you know I'll refuse to answer if you don't ask those questions?' he retorted, frowning at her.

'You don't answer personal questions or remarks. I asked you once if you were married and all you said was "I have been" in a very cold way. I got the impression you didn't want to pursue the subject.'

'I told you the truth. I have been married.' Lucas picked up the wine bottle and emptied it into their glasses.

'Is she ... is she incurable?' Kathy asked, her manner softening as she thought how awful it must have been for him when he had discovered his wife was mentally ill.

'Is who incurable?'

'Your wife.'

'I don't have a wife any more.' He picked up his glass and stood up. 'If you've had enough to eat I suggest we go into the other room and I can change the record, which seems to have finished.'

In the living room two lamps already made pools of rosy light in the purple shadows of the dark evening. Kathy chose to sit in one of the armchairs. It would be safer than the sofa, she decided. On the sofa Lucas could sit beside her and overwhelm her by sheer physical magnetism, and she didn't want to risk being close to him again. Not until she had some answers to her questions.

When he had changed the record and the sweet strains of Dvorak's Cello Concerto were whispering softly and romantically through the room he sat down on the sofa opposite her. Above the rim of his wineglass his dark eyes glittered tantalisingly at her before he drank, and she wondered if he had guessed why she had chosen to sit on a chair.

'Are you going to tell me why you don't have a wife any more?' she asked.

'She died.'

'Oh. When?'

'A couple of years ago.'

'In the mental hospital?'

Lucas set his glass down on a table at the end of the sofa and leaned towards her, his elbows on his knees.

'She was never in a mental hospital. That was some cock-and-bull story Mike Austin made up especially for your consumption, to turn you against me. I suspect he didn't want you to get too friendly with me in case I knew too much about him and told you what I knew,' he said drily.

'Perhaps you're right,' she muttered uncomfortably, remembering how willing she had been to believe Mike. 'But Jane also told me you were married, and when I asked her where your wife was she said only you and God knew and neither of you were telling, so it wasn't difficult to believe that Mike's story might be true.'

'I didn't know she had died until a few weeks

ago,' he said, studying the last of the wine in his glass. 'It's a long story, Kathy, and not a pleasant one.'

'I'd like to hear it. I think I have a right to hear it, considering . . . considering. . .' She had been going to say, 'considering our relationship', but drew back from making such a statement. After all, they didn't have a relationship of any sort whatsoever.

'Considering you and I are lovers?' suggested Lucas with a wicked glint.

'If you must put it that way, yes,' Kathy said primly, and to her annoyance he laughed.

'I have to put it that way because it's true,' he retorted. 'We were lovers nine years ago, briefly and most enjoyably. We were lovers on Friday night. It was a sudden and shocking explosive reunion. We would have been lovers again on Saturday night if Jane hadn't interfered, and we're going to be lovers tonight and many other nights stretching away into the future.'

'You're assuming too much,' she said defensively.

'I don't think so,' Lucas replied.

He leaned back. His face was now in the shadows and she realised she was sitting directly under the light. He could see her face clearly while she couldn't see his. He could watch her, study her expressions, maybe laugh at her without her knowing. As usual he had the advantage.

'Was your wife's name Mary?' she asked.

'Yes. How did you guess?'

'When did you meet her?'

'Eight years ago when I was cruising in France.'

Eight years ago. The summer he hadn't come to Redcliffe. The summer she had met Andrew.

'What was she like?' Kathy had to force herself to ask the question against the sudden upsurge of jealousy, a feeling of sheer spite that made her want to get up and leave the house rather than stay to hear more about the elusive woman Lucas had married and had, presumably, loved.

'At first she reminded me a little of you,' he said slowly. 'She had fair hair and grey eyes too, and I suppose that's why I...' He broke off, frowned and continued in a toneless voice. 'She wasn't really like you. She was older, softer, weaker, and when I met her she was down on her luck. She'd been studying painting in Paris and had fallen in love with her teacher, also an artist. He had taken her to live with him at a studio he rented in Arles in the South of France. Then he had deserted her. It was a most Bohemian story, and I suppose I should have had more sense than to get involved.'

'You felt sorry for her,' she suggested.

'I suppose I did. She was working in a gift shop trying to save up enough money to return to Scotland—she said she longed to return to her own country. So I brought her back to Edinburgh and married her, much to the disgust of my family, who didn't take to her at all.'

Kathy had a sudden vision of what his mother would be like, possessive about her handsome clever son and very jealous of any woman he might choose to marry.

'It was the biggest mistake I've ever made,' he went on bitterly. 'For a while everything was all right. I was doing well as a solicitor. Mary wasn't exactly the most marvellous housekeeper, she was too haphazard and artistic for that, but we got along fairly well together, although I couldn't say our relationship was passionate. Then about a year after we'd been married she disappeared for three months.'

'Disappeared?' Kathy felt her skin creep. The way he put it made her imagine that Mary had vanished into thin air.

'Yes. She left without telling me where she was going or why, without leaving a note. When she came back she said casually that she'd been to Paris to stay with friends. She didn't seem to care that I'd been anxious about her and had been trying to find her. Naturally I was angry, and I suppose, looking back, I did play the heavy husband. We had a pretty awful quarrel and she left again. I didn't see her for a long time.'

'But didn't you go after her and try to find her?'

'No. I was so turned off by her behaviour that I didn't bother. I was beginning to realise she didn't love me but just used me as a sort of shelter to run to when she was unhappy or down-and-out, so what little feeling I'd had for her died a natural death.' Lucas's lips curled cynically. 'I decided to let her stay away from me as long as possible so I could divorce her. She'd been gone nearly a year when I decided I'd better try to trace her so that I could go ahead with the divorce. I went to Paris and found one of her friends, who told me that when Mary had left me for the first time it was because the artist who had dumped her in Arles had asked her to go back to him. She had kept in touch with him even after she had married me.'

His voice rasped bitterly again, and he got to his feet and walked over to the record player to turn the record over.

'Did you see Mary when you were in Paris?' Kathy asked. She didn't feel jealous any more of the dead woman. Now she cared only about Lucas, empathising with him in his disillusionment.

'No. Her friend told me Mary had gone to Algeria to live with her artist lover and pleaded with me not to divorce her because she was sure Mary would come back to me when the artist dumped her again.' He broke off to set the stylus on the record. The music started up. 'And she was right,' he continued. 'Two months later Mary was back in Edinburgh, promising never to leave me again.'

'What did you do?'

He came back and sat down again on the sofa.

'By that time I'd decided to come and live down here where I could sail, and I'd managed to buy into partnership with Kelvin and Morris. Mary didn't want to come here, so a few days before I was due to move she left again. She wrote to me from Paris saying she preferred to live there.' He shrugged. 'I left it like that.'

'Did she ever come back to you?'

'Once.' His face hardened and Kathy guessed the visit had not been a successful or happy one for him. 'Not long after I'd settled in and bought this house. She didn't stay long, and while she was here she became ill and had to go into hospital.' He gave her a level glance. 'That might be where Mike Austin got the idea for the fantastic yarn he spun for you. She went into hospital in Castle Douglas for some sort of woman's complaint, and she didn't come back. When she was discharged she disappeared again. Since then I—at least until a few weeks ago—I've always been expecting her to turn up.' His lips twisted in a mirthless grin. 'The knowledge that she might turn up cramped my style a little. I couldn't make any commitment to another woman until I knew I was free of her.'

'The other night, when I knocked at your door, you said "Mary" as if you had been expecting her.'

'I know. And it was stupid of me, because I'd known for over a month that she'd died.'

'How did she die?' Kathy asked.

'Suicide. She'd gone back to her lover, but he kept deserting her, and the last time she jumped in a river somewhere and drowned.'

'How sad,' murmured Kathy. 'And how awful for a woman to be like that, to be so emotionally dependent on another person even though he treated her badly.'

'She wasn't like you,' said Lucas. 'She came from a broken home and when she was a child her emotional development was retarded through lack of attention and love. She was gentle, too gentle and submissive. She had no inner resources, no sense of independence. I think she would have been all right if I'd been able to stay with her all the time—or she would have been all right if the Frenchman could have stayed with her all the time. When each of us seemed to neglect her by going off to do our own work she ran to the other for support.'

'Why didn't you tell me all this before?' she asked.

'I didn't think I'd have to tell you at all. It was all over and Mary was dead by the time you came back on the scene. I was free to fall in love with you again. And I did.'

'Well, you didn't give me that impression!'

'Didn't I?' He was mocking her again, his lips slanting in a grin, his eyes glinting. 'Well, I wasn't going to give myself away until I could be sure you reciprocated. But when you walked into my office I felt the pull of past attraction. I felt as I hadn't felt for years, not since a moonlit night I spent once with a young woman called Kathy Warren, sharing a sleeping bag on the beach at Wreck Bay.'

'But you pretended you didn't recognise me!' she protested.

'Pretending I didn't know you made it seem like a new love affair, and I had to find ways of approaching you instead of presuming on past acquaintance,' he explained.

'You didn't hesitate to presume on past acquaintance on Friday night, making love to me without any commitment!' Kathy retorted.

'How was I to know you'd been listening to gossip about me? How was I to know you didn't trust me?' His glance raked her insolently. 'Seems to me you didn't put up much of a resistance,' he jeered.

'I didn't trust you because you'd done it once before. You made love to me at Wreck Bay without making any commitment too,' she accused.

'I told you I loved you.'

'But you didn't mean it. You went away the next day without a word.'

'So did you go away. You left Redcliffe and you weren't here when I came back.'

They were glaring and hissing at each other like two cats about to fight, both of them angry and regretful for having walked away from love and commitment nine years ago.

'Oh, I'm going to bed,' said Kathy, springing to her feet. 'I've had enough of this!'

'Suit yourself,' Lucas retorted coldly.

In the spare bedroom Kathy stood looking around. There was still time for her to leave and walk over to The Moorings. She had had the answers to her questions. She knew all about Lucas's unhappy marriage to Mary now. She knew he was free and he had told her he had fallen in love with her again.

So there was no reason why she should leave, was there? No reason why she shouldn't stay, if she wanted to. Slowly she began to undress. She put on her nightgown and dressing gown, trying to think up excuses to go downstairs again and be with Lucas.

Suddenly she remembered that she hadn't phoned her parents to tell them that she wouldn't be arriving that night. She left the bedroom and returned to the living room. Lucas was still sprawled on the sofa and the music coming from the record player was the bitter-sweet ballet *Romeo and Juliet* by Prokofiev, one of her own favourites.

'I forgot to phone my parents,' she announced, going to stand in front of Lucas. He didn't seem to be at all surprised that she had come down again, and contrarily his lack of surprise irritated her.

'The phone is over there on the desk,' he said. 'But don't make any arrangements to go to Manchester tomorrow. Now you're here you're staying.'

'Not to live with you,' she retorted. 'I've told you, I can't do that. I can't do what you want me to do.'

She went over to the desk, picked up the receiver, dialled her parents' number and waited to hear her mother's voice.

'You are going to live with me,' said Lucas autocratically, leaving the sofa and coming to stand behind her.

Kathy gave him a wary glance over her shoulder. He was close to her again, the fire at which she could warm herself for ever if she wanted; *if* she submitted to his dominance.

'I want you, Kathy,' he murmured. 'I've always wanted you, but we were separated by circumstances beyond our control.'

'We're not Romeo and Juliet any more,' she whispered. 'We're both older, experienced. . .'

'Knowledgeable, so it will be better,' he suggested. 'It's been better already,' he added, moving closer, his dark glance slanting to her lips and just then her mother spoke.

'Mother, Kathy here.' She turned away from him. 'I'm sorry, I should have called you before. I won't be arriving this evening as planned. . .'

'We had noticed, Kathy.' There was a sort of weary patience in the tone of Hilda Warren's voice as if she were accustomed to her children not arriving at the time they had said they would. 'It's nearly ten o'clock. You said you'd be here about nine.'

'Oh, is it? I hadn't realised. I hope you haven't been worrying.'

'We have, but that goes without saying. Where are you?'

'Still in Redcliffe. Something came up and I've been delayed.'

Two hands slid around her waist and curved upwards to her breasts. Against the side of her neck Lucas's lips were hot and his teeth nipped sharply. She felt her pulses leap and shivers of desire tingled through her. She hardly heard what her mother said and had to ask her to repeat.

'I said shall we expect you tomorrow?' shouted Hilda Warren.

The hands at her breasts tightened and she was pulled back against Lucas's hard body.

'Tell her no or you'll be sorry,' he whispered tauntingly in her ear, and bit the lobe.

'N-no, I . . . I'll phone you again and let you know what I'm going to do. I may stay here until I've sold Seaview.'

'All right, then, dear. We'll expect to hear from you later in the week. Goodbye.'

Lucas's hands were withdrawn. He moved away from her. Kathy said goodbye to her mother, heard the phone go down at the other end of the line and put the receiver back on its rest. For a few moments she stood there, trying to control the waves of desire that were surging through her, then slowly she turned and went to sit on the sofa by Lucas, who was lounging back looking for all the world as if he hadn't moved from that place.

'Are you going to sell Seaview?' he asked casually.

'Do you want to buy it?'

'If I did I'd knock it down, you realise that, don't you? It does obstruct the view from this house of the river,' he said. 'You might not like it if I did that.'

If the cottage was knocked down her last link with Andrew would be destroyed. But then if she sold it to someone else the link with Andrew would be gone too.

'I don't know what to do,' she muttered.

'So forget it for a while. You don't have to decide yet what to do with it. There's no hurry.'

Another silence. Kathy could hear her own heart quicken its beat, her own breath coming faster. In her lap her hands twisted together.

'Lucas?' she queried at last.

'Mmm?'

'You said you phoned Kenny and he came and took Jane away with him. Does that mean your affair with her is over?'

'What affair? I've never had an affair with Jane,' he retorted.

'Well, some of the people in the village think you have, and she has known you a long time and...'

'She's pursued me,' he cut in disgustedly. 'And I've always managed to keep her at arm's length by telling her that I was married to Mary.' He turned to her. The glance of his dark blue eyes was warm and sensual and when he raised a hand to touch her throat ripples of desire quivered through her. 'Tonight Jane was lying when she said Kenny had left her. It was she who walked out on him after they'd had a row about me. The only way I could put her off this time was to tell her I'm going to marry you.'

'But... but I thought... I supposed that after your experience with Mary you might not be interested in marriage,' Kathy whispered, not looking at him. 'You seem so wary of making any commitment.'

'That's true—I am,' he admitted. 'But if it's commitment you want from me before you'll stay here and live with me, Kathy, I'll apply for a special licence tomorrow and we can be married very soon.'

His fingers slid along her collarbone and he eased the dressing gown from her shoulder. Against the vulnerable hollow between neck and shoulder he had exposed his lips burned.

'You're sure?' she whispered.

'I'm very sure.' He raised his head. Little fires blazed in the dark depths of his eyes. 'I was sure nine years ago, but it didn't work out, and it's always been there, buried deep inside me, the feeling that I'd been cheated out of what was really mine by not being able to marry you. When John Reid used to talk about you and Andrew I used to feel mad with jealousy, mad enough to throttle Andrew if ever I should meet him because he'd been able to marry you and I hadn't. Kathy, will you marry me as soon as possible?'

'I don't know if I can. It's too soon after Andrew's death,' she protested.

'Yet I'm sure you're as much in love with me as I am with you,' Lucas argued, his voice rasping. 'You've always been in love with me but, like I did, you buried your feelings for me when we didn't meet again and tried to forget. You let your damned stubborn pride come between us and married Andrew instead.'

'Well, so did you—so did you!' she cried out accusingly. 'You married Mary.'

'Because I couldn't have you, and unlike you she seemed to need me. And you married Andrew for the same reason.'

Kathy thought about that and had to admit he was right. She had married Andrew because he had needed her, and he had been only a substitute for her real love, Lucas, and that was why her marriage to him had been so unfulfilled, so lacking in passion.

'But I did love Andrew,' she whispered forlornly.

'Not like you loved and still love me,' he retorted arrogantly. 'Not with passion and beyond reason.'

He moved close to her, encircling her with that magic power he possessed. Taking her head between his hands, he began to kiss her, raining kisses on her cheeks, her eyes, her lips so that she had no breath left to argue or disagree with him.

The dressing gown slid away from her and his hands probed the silkiness of her nightgown. He lifted her across his knees and as his lips began to maraud her face again she heard the fabric of her nightgown tear with a faint hiss as he tore the bodice. Desire blazed up in her and she returned his kisses hungrily, her lips seeking and finding the sweet wine flavour of his.

'Can you say now that you don't love me?' he whispered thickly. 'Can you say now that it's too soon after Andrew? Somehow I don't think you can. Somehow I don't believe he ever took my place. I was your first lover and I'm going to make sure I'm going to be your next lover and possibly your last. I'm not going to let you escape again. And if you dare to leave tomorrow I'm going to follow you wherever you go. I'm going to hound you until you give in and agree to live with me for the rest of our lives.'

He didn't give her a chance to reply but covered her lips with another sense-inflaming kiss. Dark primitive hungers were unleashed within her at the touch of his fingers on her skin. Twisting against him in abandon, she pulled at the opening of his shirt. Her hands slid over the breadth of his chest, her fingers curling to the crispness of hairs.

'Do you still want to go to bed?' he asked huskily.

'Yes.' It came out in a groan of frustration because after all her response to his demands he had stopped caressing her.

'Alone? In the spare bedroom?' he queried, tormenting her.

'No. With you. With you!' she moaned, clinging to him unashamedly. 'Carry me there. Carry me!'

With a soft laugh Lucas lunged to his feet, still holding her, and carried her through to his bedroom where the lamps were already lit and the covers had been turned back as if in readiness for their coming. Seeing the lit lamps, the turned-down bed as evidence of his assumption that he would be bringing her to that room, Kathy couldn't help but tease him.

'Looks as if you were expecting someone to sleep with you tonight!'

'I was. You,' he replied, putting her down on the bed.

'You're very self-confident, very arrogant,' she sniped.

'Always,' he agreed aggravatingly.

He turned away from her to take off his clothes. Lying back, Kathy admired the shape of his legs, the ripple of muscles in his back.

'Supposing I'd gone to bed upstairs? Supposing I hadn't come down to make that phone call?' she challenged.

'Then I'd have come to you and we'd have had to manage in one of the twin beds,' he replied. 'Much better to be here,' he whispered, sliding into bed beside her.

Long arms hauled her against his nakedness.

Then her nightgown was gone and his bare skin was rubbing hers in subtle sense-arousing movements. In her hair his hands were ruthless as he tipped her head back and ravaged her face and throat with stinging kisses.

'You're very eager,' she gasped when she found breath.

'But you like it. And you need it. You need to be roused, Kathy, out of that romantic sleep in which you've been indulging yourself. You need to be prodded alive like this and like this.' He pinched and poked at her until she cried out and reached blindly for him. 'It's only when you're roused that you forget to be stiff and self-protective. It's only then that you drop your armour and let love rush in and take over.'

'Oh, I love you. I love you, Lucas,' she sighed, grasping hold of him and pulling him down on top of her.

He became still then. Lifting his head, he looked down at her.

'And you'll stay and we'll start planning our life together?' he queried seriously. 'It isn't just for making love I want you. I want far more than that from you and I want to give you more than that. I want us to be friends and partners as well as lovers, so will you marry me?'

'Yes, yes!' She moved beneath him, tempting with gentle seductive undulations of her body while her hands slid caressingly over his back.

'And we'll have a family?' he persisted, still holding back.

'Do you want children?' she asked in surprise. She had never thought of him as a father. The selfish type, Polly Travis had called him. But then why should she consider Polly's or anyone else's opinion of him any more? Polly didn't know him very well. Neither did Mike Austin. And she herself was only just beginning to know a little about him; beginning to learn about the depth of his passion for herself.

'Don't you?' he asked, and she sensed again he had withdrawn again, warily.

'Oh, yes, I do—I do,' she replied fervently. 'A boy with black hair and blue eyes.'

'A girl with sea-grey eyes,' retorted Lucas, his mouth slanted in its slow smile. 'So what are we waiting for now, my long-lost, newly found lover? What are we waiting for?'

'This,' Kathy whispered, flinging her arms about him joyously, and forgetting to be stiff and self-protective, she let his love for her rush in and take over.

Coming Next Month in Harlequin Presents!

855 A FOREVER AFFAIR Rosemary Carter
Despite its savage beauty, her husband's African game reserve is no longer home. Was it carved in stone that she could never love another man? Surely a divorce would change that!

856 PROMISE OF THE UNICORN Sara Craven
To collect on a promise, a young woman returns her talisman—the protector of virgins—to its original owner. The power of the little glass unicorn was now with him!

857 AN IRRESISTIBLE FORCE Ann Charlton
A young woman is in danger of being taken over by a subtle irresistible force rather than by open aggression when she takes on an Australian construction king who's trying to buy out her grandmother.

858 INNOCENT PAWN Catherine George
Instead of looking past the money to the man behind it, a mother is prompted by panic to blame her husband when their five-year-old daughter is kidnapped.

859 MALIBU MUSIC Rosemary Hammond
California sunshine and her sister's beach house provide the atmosphere a young woman needs to focus on her future—until her neighbor tries to seduce her.

860 LADY SURRENDER Carole Mortimer
The man who bursts into her apartment can't see why his best friend would throw away his marriage for a woman like her. But soon he can't imagine any man—married or otherwise—*not* falling for her.

861 A MODEL OF DECEPTION Margaret Pargeter
A model takes on an assignment she can't handle when she tries to entice a man into selling his island in the Caribbean. She was supposed to deceive the man, not fall in love.

862 THE HAWK OF VENICE Sally Wentworth
Most people travel to Venice to fall in love. Instead, an au pair girl makes the journey to accuse a respected Venetian count of kidnapping—or of seduction, at least.

Here's how to get this special offer from Harlequin!
As simple as 1…2…3!

SEPTEMBER
TREASURY EDITION
COUPON

1. Each month, save one Treasury Edition coupon from your favorite Romance or Presents novel.
2. In four months you'll have saved four Treasury Edition coupons (<u>only one coupon</u> per month allowed).
3. Then all you have to do is fill out and return the order form provided, along with the four Treasury Edition coupons required and $1.00 for postage and handling.

Mail to: Harlequin Reader Service

In the U.S.A.
2504 West Southern Ave.
Tempe, AZ 85282

In Canada
P.O. Box 2800, Postal Station A
5170 Yonge Street
Willowdale, Ont. M2N 6J3

RT1-B-2

Please send me my FREE copy of the Janet Dailey Treasury Edition. I have enclosed the four Treasury Edition coupons required and $1.00 for postage and handling along with this order form.

(Please Print)

NAME_____

ADDRESS_____

CITY_____

STATE/PROV._____ ZIP/POSTAL CODE_____

SIGNATURE_____
This offer is limited to one order per household.

SUPPLIES LIMITED

This special Janet Dailey offer expires January 1986.